HAMMERHAL

D1196382

More Warhammer from Black Library

HALLOWED KNIGHTS: PLAGUE GARDEN
Josh Reynolds

EIGHT LAMENTATIONS: SPEAR OF SHADOWS
Josh Reynolds

OVERLORDS OF THE IRON DRAGON
C L Werner

CITY OF SECRETS
Nick Horth

WARHAMMER®
CHRONICLES

• **THE LEGEND OF SIGMAR** •
Graham McNeill
BOOK ONE: Heldenhammer
BOOK TWO: Empire
BOOK THREE: God King

• **THE RISE OF NAGASH** •
Mike Lee
BOOK ONE: Nagash the Sorcerer
BOOK TWO: Nagash the Unbroken
BOOK THREE: Nagash Immortal

• **THE VAMPIRE WARS** •
Steven Savile
BOOK ONE: Inheritance
BOOK TWO: Dominion
BOOK THREE: Retribution

• **THE SUNDERING** •
Gav Thorpe
BOOK ONE: Malekith
BOOK TWO: Shadow King
BOOK THREE: Caledor

• **CHAMPIONS OF CHAOS** •
Darius Hinks, Sarah Cawkwell &
Ben Counter
BOOK ONE: Sigvald
BOOK TWO: Valkia the Bloody
BOOK THREE: Van Horstmann

HAMMERHAL

Josh Reynolds

BLACK LIBRARY

A BLACK LIBRARY PUBLICATION

First published in Great Britain in 2017 by
Black Library
This edition published in Great Britain in 2018 by
Black Library,
Games Workshop Ltd.,
Willow Road,
Nottingham,
NG7 2WS, UK.

10 9 8 7 6 5 4 3 2 1

Produced by Games Workshop in Nottingham.
Cover illustration by Akim Kaliberda.

A CIP record for this book is available from the British Library.

ISBN 13: 978-1-78496-750-5

See Black Library on the internet at

blacklibrary.com

Find out more about Games Workshop
and the worlds of Warhammer at

games-workshop.com

Printed and bound by CPI Group (UK) Ltd, Croydon, CR0 4YY

From the maelstrom of a sundered world, the
Eight Realms were born. The formless and the divine
exploded into life.

Strange, new worlds appeared in the firmament, each one
gilded with spirits, gods and men. Noblest of the gods was
Sigmar. For years beyond reckoning he illuminated the realms,
wreathed in light and majesty as he carved out his reign. His
strength was the power of thunder. His wisdom was infinite.
Mortal and immortal alike kneeled before his lofty throne.
Great empires rose and, for a while, treachery was banished.
Sigmar claimed the land and sky as his own and ruled over a
glorious age of myth.

But cruelty is tenacious. As had been foreseen, the great
alliance of gods and men tore itself apart. Myth and legend
crumbled into Chaos. Darkness flooded the realms. Torture,
slavery and fear replaced the glory that came before. Sigmar
turned his back on the mortal kingdoms, disgusted by their
fate. He fixed his gaze instead on the remains of the world he
had lost long ago, brooding over its charred core, searching
endlessly for a sign of hope. And then, in the dark heat of
his rage, he caught a glimpse of something magnificent. He
pictured a weapon born of the heavens. A beacon powerful
enough to pierce the endless night. An army hewn from
everything he had lost.

Sigmar set his artisans to work and for long ages they toiled,
striving to harness the power of the stars. As Sigmar's great
work neared completion, he turned back to the realms and saw
that the dominion of Chaos was almost complete. The hour
for vengeance had come. Finally, with lightning blazing across
his brow, he stepped forth to unleash his creations.

The Age of Sigmar had begun.

PROLOGUE

DARK GOD'S LAUGHTER

The divine consciousness of Sigmar Heldenhammer, the God-King, raced down from the celestial peaks of Azyr and into the tangled canopies of Ghyran, the Realm of Life. His awareness, shrouded in storm winds and rain, descended through vast clouds of floating spores, passing by the shattered husks of sky-islands and storm-reefs to the green lands below.

Ghyran was a vibrant realm. Life was everywhere, taking innumerable shapes. It grew and spread with a hunger that defied all logic, responding to the eternal song of Alarielle the Everqueen. He could hear her voice echoing from every corner of her realm, as the Goddess of Life tried to put right all that was wrong and heal the wounds of war. But there were places that even her song could not reach. Places where other, darker gods held sway.

In moments, the Nevergreen Mountains rose wild about him. Sigmar was there and yet not there, a shard of his godly might riding a storm wind through the dark pine reaches of the Hexwood, which covered the mountains' slopes.

Gradually the wind coalesced, joining with the light of the stars and the sound of distant thunder to assume the seeming of a man, clad in golden war-plate embossed with celestial heraldry. It was a form the God-King had taken often, in days gone by, when the Mortal Realms were at peace and the gods were of one mind, united in a pantheon.

But all things ended. One by one, the gods had abandoned Sigmar's grand alliance, or betrayed him. The embers of an old, familiar anger flared at the thought, and thunder rumbled somewhere over the mountain peaks. Even Alarielle had retreated at last, withdrawing deep into the hidden glades of Ghyran, there to sleep and dream.

And as the old alliances shattered, war had rocked the Mortal Realms to their very roots. The Ruinous Powers – the four Dark Gods of Chaos – pressed close about the threshold of reality, and no realm save his own had been safe from their attentions.

Ghyran had seen more than its share of that conflict. The Plague God, Nurgle, had claimed it as his own, turning the rampant creation to stagnation. But the servants of the Everqueen had fought alongside Sigmar's own, if grudgingly, and had beaten the foetid servants of Nurgle back on several fronts, weakening the Plague God's hold on the realm.

Nevertheless, where one of the Dark Gods weakened, the others grew strong. That was the nature of the Ruinous Powers. They waged war on each other as readily as on Sigmar or the other gods of the Mortal Realms. And where Nurgle found himself stymied, his great rival Tzeentch, the God of Change, was sure to seek some advantage.

And here, in the Nevergreen Mountains, the Architect of Fate was making his move. Sigmar could sense the innumerable skeins of possibility and chance weaving through the Hexwood. Every tree in the forest thrummed with corruption. Each one seemed to be a black wound in reality, and past them he could see cancerous pathways stretching away somewhere, beyond even his sight.

Something vast and monstrous waited here, just beyond the trees, watching him. It had foreseen his arrival, and its laughter itched at the back of his mind like a nagging ache. A susurrus of muttering pursued him as he moved on, teasing and taunting him. He longed to face the laughing presence that he knew to be Tzeentch as he might once have. In those early days, he had matched his might against that of the Ruinous Powers, but he'd come to learn through harsh experience that there was no profit in such a confrontation. So instead, he ignored it and continued on, speeding through the forest, faster now, seeking what had drawn his attention, even in high Sigmaron in his home realm of Azyr.

He felt the touch of a mind, much like his own, start in recognition as his consciousness entered a wide clearing. Twisted trees rose up like the crumbled parapets of a broken citadel, casting strange shadows across the bestial shapes cavorting beneath their branches. The beastkin reeked of Tzeentch; his corrupting touch was obvious upon them. The tzaangors were avian-featured and horned, bedecked in savage totems and bearing weapons of bone, iron and crystal. Some of them had once been men, before the magics of Tzeentch had twisted them into new, more awful shapes. Others had been born mere beasts, raised up by foul rites to walk on two legs rather than four.

Whatever their origin, the beastkin capered to the dissonant music of crouched drummers and whirling pipers, screeching and howling in time to the cacophony. The trees about the clearing seemed to flex and bend with the raucous noise, their bark blistering beneath the caress of the damnable incense rising from the multi-coloured bonfires which littered the clearing.

At its heart, a blister of crystalline rock sprouted from the soil. It was a flux-cairn – a sour growth of stagnant magics, raised by the servants of Tzeentch to honour their dark master and facilitate his endless schemes. It spread like a gangrenous crown, its milky facets catching the light in eerie ways. The formation of fossilised sorcery towered over the tzaangors and reverberated with the thumping of their drums. Motes of iridescence, which Sigmar knew to be captured magics, crawled through it like fireflies.

The flux-cairn was the foul heart of the forest, the darkling pathways hidden within the trees all stretching unseen through its facets and into unknown realms beyond. Sigmar could feel the twisted paths growing, stretching towards their destination. The sensation of it was like the hum of a mosquito in his skull, or an itch he could not scratch. He desired nothing more than to destroy the cairn, to call down the lightning which was his to command and shatter it into a million pieces.

But something stayed his hand. He gazed deeper into the heart of the flux-cairn, and that was when he saw them: silvery spheres, wrapped in something that might have been vines or algae, hanging suspended within the cairn.

'Soulpods,' he murmured.

The newborn seedlings of Alarielle's favoured servants: the sylvaneth.

The soulpods throbbed with potential – they were the raw stuff of life, waiting for their moment to bloom and grow. Within them, tree-kin spirits – though of what sort Sigmar could not say – waited for their rebirth and clamoured for release. They flickered within their cage of crystal. They sensed him, and their unformed consciousness stretched out towards him, imploring him for aid.

Aid he could not give them. This place was not his, and already he could feel the Everqueen's anger at his presence growing. She had sensed him the moment he had entered Ghyran unannounced, and had raced with the winds to confront him. He felt her anger at his intrusion wash over him like the heat of a summer's day.

In an attempt to forestall her fury, he asked, 'How long have they been captives, sister?'

'Too long, Thunderer.' Alarielle's voice scraped across his consciousness like the sting of a hundred nettles. Her seeming appeared before him in a swirl of loose leaves and pollen. Teeth made from thorns were bared in a snarl of challenge. 'It is no concern of yours, Lord of the Heavens. Leave this place and seek your own battles.'

Though it was his servants who had helped weaken the Dark Gods' hold on Ghyran, Sigmar knew that Alarielle bore him little love. Perhaps she still blamed him for failures of old, or perhaps the war-song now beat so strongly within her that she could not perceive help when it was freely offered. Either way, he was reluctant to test the fragile bonds of their current alliance. And yet he could not bring himself to depart.

'What is happening here, sister? Perhaps I can be of help...'

She swelled with wrath at his words, her form expanding to gigantic proportions, invisible to the mortal eye but unsettling nonetheless. Like Sigmar, her physical manifestation was elsewhere, engaged in some other conflict. But this shard of her was potent enough.

'I need no aid. This is my place. My realm. Not yours.'

He could feel a familiar rage boiling within her. Long years of hardship had worn her patience to less than nothing. She longed to strike at the enemy as he himself did – to drive them before her and cast their corpses into the deepest pits. Her anger was like a hurricane beating against his perception. He drew back, lest it draw him in.

Around them, tzaangors sniffed the air and squawked nervously. They could not discern either god, but some magical sense, gifted to them by their twisted patron, had alerted them that something was amiss. The air was alive with magics.

Sigmar turned. The bowers and glens of the forest echoed with screams. He heard blades sink noisily into wood. Flesh was being torn by splintery claws, and bone snapped within constricting coils of vine. Something was coming.

'I merely came to offer my aid,' he began again, but Alarielle flung out a claw of pine needles and blossoms, silencing him.

'My children have arrived. They come, and this farce ends.'

With an ear-splitting shriek, the sylvaneth erupted into the clearing. The tree-kin were bark-covered nightmares, with splintery jaws and branch-like talons. They resembled humans, but only at a distance. Some towered over their companions, swinging blades made from fossilised wood and rock. Others bore no weapons save their claws. They fell upon the tzaangors like the rage of the Everqueen made manifest. The beastkin screeched and fought back, trying to protect the flux-cairn.

The battle was fierce. Sigmar watched as a titanic sylvaneth swung a tzaangor about by its horn, smashing it to a bloody paste against the ground. The gleaming falchions and spears of the tzaangors drew sap from the twisting bodies of the tree-kin. The battle swung one way, and then the other. For every tzaangor that fell, two more raced to take its place, yet the sylvaneth fought with a fury that the beastkin could not match. The soulpods were their future, and they would risk almost anything to save them.

The air pulsed with Alarielle's war-song as the Everqueen urged her children on. The wordless harmony rose and fell with the wind whipping between the trees, driving the sylvaneth to greater effort. Then, all at once, a shriek echoed through the glen.

Sigmar saw a hideous figure clamber atop the flux-cairn, staff in hand. This tzaangor wore ragged robes, and its thin form was bedecked with totems and sorcerous fetishes. It was a shaman, a wielder of twisted magics. It slammed the ferrule of its staff down against the top of the cairn, and the crystalline facets flashed with silent, sickly lightning.

The soulpods screamed. Their cry, part fear and part pain, echoed through the minds of every living thing in the clearing. Whatever the shaman was doing, it was hurting the nascent spirits. Alarielle echoed their cry, and her anger shook the clearing to its roots. The trees wept leaves, and the ground ruptured. The flux-cairn itself shook, and more lightning flashed as the soulpods within continued to wail.

The tzaangor shaman screeched meaningfully.

The threat was plain, obvious even to the most bloodthirsty soul. The sylvaneth were prepared to risk themselves, but not the very thing they'd come to save. The tree-kin retreated, slowly at first, and then more quickly. They slipped away, vanishing into the gloom, as the tzaangor screeched and howled in celebration of their victory.

Alarielle watched in silence, her earlier rage gone as quickly as it had come. Her seeming shrank into itself, her gaze fixed upon the flux-cairn and its prisoners. They called to her, but she could not answer them. She turned to look at Sigmar, her expression unreadable. She would not ask for aid. Could not. He understood – it was not the way of a god to beg aid from another.

'Sister, let me help you,' he said. He held out his hand. 'As I have done before, let me do so now. Together, we might…'

But her seeming was gone. Like a morning mist, it wavered and dispersed, taking her attentions with it. There were other battles to be fought elsewhere that demanded her attentions. Ghyran shook with the drumbeat of war. This battle was lost; others might yet be won.

Sigmar let his hand drop. Weariness stole over him. Once, Alarielle would not have hesitated to accept his aid. Once, he and the other gods would have come to her aid unasked.

But those days were long past. The pantheon was dust, and less than dust.

He looked up, seeking relief in the stars. Azyr. The Celestial Realm. *His* realm. The last true bulwark against the depredations of the Ruinous Powers. He had his own wars to fight, his own realm to defend. If the other gods did not desire his help, he would leave them to it, for good or ill. But as he made ready to depart, he heard again the laughter of Tzeentch ringing out of the hidden places, taunting him.

Thunder rumbled overhead, and the laughter fell momentarily silent. The celestial lightning coiled about Sigmar as the old anger flared fully now. It was never far from the surface. He was a tempest wrought in the shape of a man. His hair and beard were as swirling black clouds, and his eyes were full of lightning. His face became a swirl of stars, blazing with cold light. His voice boomed like thunder as he bellowed a challenge into the teeth of the laughter. He was the first storm and the last, the storm which would wash the filth of Chaos from the Mortal Realms forever.

He lowered his hands, and the lightning calmed its writhing. The stars retreated, and the tempest with them, leaving only the cold edge of determination behind. The stars shone bright overhead, and he knew what he must do.

As he had done before, he would do now. And the Dark Gods be damned.

CHAPTER ONE

THE TWIN-TAILED CITY

The rat chittered, exposing yellow incisors in warning. Belloc growled and tossed his knife. The rat fled as the narrow blade thudded into the side of a mould-encrusted crate. The dock-warden cursed and ambled to retrieve his weapon. As he did so, he saw the flash of eyes in the nearby shadows. The rat wasn't alone. They never were. Where there was one, there were a dozen – these days, at least. The sacks of grain that were stacked along the causeway of the aether-dock were irresistible to hungry vermin.

The docks rose high over Hammerhal's warehouse district, one ring of berths and warehouses stacked atop the next, almost all the way up its length. From each ring, an ever-spreading canopy of high-altitude berths and quays extended out over the tangled streets below, like branches stretching from a tree of immense size.

Belloc had heard that it was, in fact, just that – that much of the city had been grown rather than built. He didn't know whether he believed that or not, though there were stranger things in this realm, to be sure.

Hammerhal itself, for instance. The Twin-tailed City stretched across two of the eight Mortal Realms, separated by untold infinities thanks to the Stormrift Realmgate. Like all realmgates, it was a portal through which one could pass into another realm entirely. Countless numbers of these apertures in reality were scattered about the Mortal Realms, and all of the great cities were built about one or more realmgates.

Hammerhal spread outwards from the twinned thresholds of the Stormrift Realmgate into both Ghyran, the Realm of Life, and Aqshy, the Realm of Fire. Belloc had only been to Hammerhal Aqsha once, and the experience hadn't been a pleasant one. The air had tasted of cinders and smoke, and he'd been covered in sweat from sunup to sundown. Ghyran was better, but not by much – it was too wet here, too humid. He missed Azyr. The Celestial Realm had its problems, but at least the weather was pleasant.

He plucked his knife free of the crate and spun it lightly between his fingers, careful not to cut himself.

'Well,' he said, glaring at the rats, 'anything to say for yourselves?'

When no reply was forthcoming, he kicked the mouldering crate towards them. It came apart as his boot touched it, and he yelped in disgust. Bits and pieces clattered across the ground, and the rats took the hint, scattering into the shadows.

Belloc hopped back, scraping at the sludge on his boot with the edge of his knife. If it got into the leather, he would have to get new boots, and he'd only just managed to break these ones in. He looked around as he dislodged the last of it. There was mould everywhere, growing on every warehouse and berth that occupied the vast wooden platform of the docks. And vines. And weeds, even. It seemed inconceivable that anything should be growing this high above the city proper, but life found a way. Especially in Hammerhal Ghyra.

This side of the bifurcated city was awash in unwelcome

growth. The heat from the Fire-Bastions could only do so much; no matter how much lava was channelled into the immense stone runnels from Hammerhal Aqsha, the city's spires and golden domes were under eternal siege from Ghyran's excessively exuberant plant life.

And the rats. Always the rats.

'Vermin,' Belloc muttered, thrusting his knife back into its sheath.

That was all this job was, at times. The dock-warden scratched at his unshaven chin. He was burly, but not especially brave, even with a sword on his hip. He wasn't ashamed. Bravery cost extra, and the owners of the docks were notoriously cheap. You got what you paid for, and they had paid for Belloc. Luckily, no one was stupid enough to climb all the way up here, just to filch grain – or worse, try and steal an airship. So it was just him and the rats.

He wondered if Delph and the others were as bored as he was. Probably. Things were either boring or terrifying this high up, but they had drawn the short straws and been forced to patrol the uppermost ring.

He didn't like it up here. The Kharadron vessels smelled of strange chemicals and the vibrations of their buoyancy endrins shook the entire dock. The sky-duardin were a stand-offish folk who kept to themselves, unless they had business to attend to. He'd heard from Delph that they lived in flying cities, but didn't know how much credence there was in that.

Then again, Delph was a duardin herself, so perhaps she'd know, if anyone did. She said the Kharadron were duardin who had retreated to the skies when the armies of the Dark Gods had swept over the Mortal Realms. She didn't seem to like them very much. Granted, she didn't like anyone.

Belloc stared at one of the Kharadron vessels. It was oddly shaped. Too many curves. The bulbous aether-endrins that held the ship aloft glowed dimly, even when at anchor. If you stared at them for too long, you got dizzy. Belloc blinked and looked away.

There were sounds up here too, sometimes. Not the usual creaking and groaning you'd expect, but something else. Smells, too – acrid and unpleasant. Once, he thought he'd seen something watching him from the roof of a warehouse.

Suddenly uneasy, he glanced at the unfamiliar stars above. The sky was green here, even now at night, with the faintest tinge of azure. Sometimes it was so pale it was almost white, and sometimes it was so dark as to be black, but it was always a shade of green. The stars were the worst. They were the same as in Azyr, he was certain, but somehow different, as if he were looking at them from the wrong angle.

He blinked and tore his eyes away from the unforgiving sky. Beyond the obscuring wall of anchored airships and skycutters, Hammerhal Ghyra stretched across the horizon. It was almost beautiful from up here. Parts of the city were given over to vast groves of trees, and amongst the green he could see golden domes and white towers rising over a sea of smaller buildings.

A constant flow of molten rock poured down through immense stone and crystal runnels that emerged from the city's heart, where the Stormrift Realmgate was located. The glowing lines stretched like veins through the tangled streets towards the distant defensive canals which marked the outer districts. He could just make out the faint reddish glow of the Fire-Bastions on the horizon.

Each time the city extended its borders, the Fire-Bastions were duly redirected by teams of human and duardin artisans. The engineers of the Ironweld Arsenal were capable of great feats of artifice. They bent the wisdom of two races towards devising weapons and mechanisms for the reconquest of the Mortal Realms.

The Fire-Bastions were one such mechanism. Fed by the runnels of molten rock, they served to burn back the ravenous flora of the realm, keeping the outer districts of the city from being overwhelmed by fast-growing plant life.

The hollow, ashen network of tunnels that were left behind when the Fire-Bastions were redirected were then gradually built over and hidden from sight. Belloc sometimes wondered how many of those tunnels were repurposed rather than filled in, and how many still ran beneath the winding streets of Hammerhal Ghyra.

'And probably rats in all of them,' he muttered.

The city was full of rats. And worse things. No one talked about it, but that didn't mean it wasn't so. He'd left Azyrheim one step ahead of the thief-takers, but a stretch in the sky-cages didn't seem so bad now compared to some of the things he'd seen.

Delph and the others swore blind that the mystic wards around the city prevented anything too horrible from getting in. They said the magic kept the monsters out, but Belloc wasn't concerned about the ones outside. He was more worried about the ones that might already be in the city somewhere. Hiding. *Waiting*.

There were stories. There were always stories, even in Azyrheim. About rats that walked on two legs, and men with the heads of goats and wolf's teeth. Belloc was no child. He knew that monsters were real, and their gods too. And he knew that nothing could keep them out for long, if they were truly of a mind to get in.

As he gazed at the horizon, he found his eyes drawn towards the Nevergreen Mountains. He'd never seen them up close, but he'd heard about the great forest that covered their broken slopes and the things that lurked within it. Lightning flashed, arcing between the distant peaks and the night sky. He shivered. The lightning reminded him that the Stormcast Eternals had marched west, towards the mountains, two days before.

He shivered again, thinking of those massive, silver-clad warriors as they passed through the steaming gates of the Fire-Bastions. Delph said they'd been human once, before Sigmar had blessed them with divine strength and holy armour, but what would a duardin know about such things? She didn't even worship Sigmar. Like most duardin – at least those he knew – she worshipped Grungni, the god of her folk.

Something clattered. Belloc froze. Then, slowly, he turned.

It was probably a rat. It was almost certainly a rat. But sometimes it wasn't. He'd heard stories that sometimes things crawled down out of the green sky, looking for food. It was the same in Azyrheim, but it was somehow worse here. He reached for the hilt of his sword as he took a step towards where the sound had originated from – an alleyway between two warehouses.

Belloc didn't call for help. Delph had gotten angry the last time he'd called for help and there hadn't been any need. He needed this job. Besides, if it was something other than a rat, calling for help would only attract its attention all the quicker.

He took a step towards the alleyway. For a moment, he heard only the creak of rigging and the whistle of the wind blowing between the buildings. Warehouses of all sizes clustered thick here, near the edge of the ring, and they collected shadows.

Another clatter, and a rat ran out of the alleyway, squealing.

Belloc sighed in relief. He nearly choked on that sigh as something pounced on the rat. The rodent died instantly as four dun paws crushed it flat. A tawny, feathered skull dipped, and a hooked beak tore at its kill. Belloc took a step back. The thing turned, golden eyes fixed on him.

'Gryph-hound,' he muttered as a chill raced along his spine. The creature resembled a small lion, only with the head of a bird of prey. It was no larger than a wolf, but it was far more lethal. Its tail lashed as it crouched over its kill. He held out his hands and began to back away slowly. 'Easy there. No harm done. Enjoy your meal.'

It might have come off one of the airships, but there was no way to tell. Just as he was about to call out for help, he bumped into someone. An instant later, something very sharp was resting against his neck.

'Hello, friend,' said a voice. 'No, don't move. Especially don't try to draw that sword you're wearing. Things might take an unfortunate turn.'

Belloc kept his hands from his blade. *Thieves*, he thought. Or worse. He made to speak, but the pressure of the blade against his throat increased slightly.

'Quietly, friend. Quietly. No need to speak.'

Belloc quickly closed his mouth.

'Good,' continued the voice. 'Good. Now, I need you to point out the berth belonging to the sky-merchant Rollo Tarn. Remember, don't reach for the sword.'

Tarn? Why did they want Tarn? He didn't ship anything valuable. Just wood. Belloc's mind spun in confusion. No one could expect him to die for wood, could they? He gestured slowly, hesitantly. The pressure of the knife was removed, and he sucked in a breath.

'There now. Excellent. That wasn't so difficult, was it?'

Belloc swallowed, but didn't reply. He was too busy praying.

'You can turn around, now.'

Belloc did. The man before him was tall, and dressed like someone with more sense than to be creeping around the aether-docks at night. He wore a heavy, triple-caped overcoat over something that might have once been the uniform of a Freeguild warrior. A basket-hilted rapier was sheathed on one hip, and he had a brace of pistols on the other. On the lapel of his coat was pinned a symbol that Belloc recognised all too well from his time in Azyrheim: the hammer and comet of the Order of Azyr.

Belloc drew back in fear.

'Witch hunter!'

CHAPTER TWO

SERVANTS OF AZYR

Sol Gage, knight of the Order of Azyr, sighed, reversed the knife he held and forcefully tapped his prisoner on the head with its weighted pommel. The dock-warden crumpled without a sound, and the witch hunter lowered him gently to the ground. He sheathed his knife.

'Bryn,' he said, 'get him out of sight.'

'Couldn't have thumped him in here, then?' a deep voice growled querulously. A squat, heavy form stumped from out of the shadows behind Gage. Thick hands caught the unconscious dock-warden by the ankles, and began to drag him away.

'I'm sorry, my friend – I thought you might be bored.' As Gage spoke, a second shape, much taller than the witch hunter, stepped over the dock-warden's body. Gage glanced up into a stern yet noble countenance, wrought in silver. 'Don't scowl so, Carus. I didn't kill him.'

'I am not scowling.'

Carus Iron-Oath stood head and shoulders above even the

tallest of mortal men. Clad in silver war-plate forged from holy sigmarite, the Lord-Veritant of the Hallowed Knights was an imposing sight. A cloak of deep azure hung from his shoulders, and dark eyes peered out from behind his war-mask, the only sign of the man within.

No, not just a man, Gage reminded himself. A Stormcast Eternal – one of Sigmar's chosen warriors, forged anew on the Anvil of Apotheosis and made into something better. Or, at least, something stronger. Where most Stormcasts were warriors first and foremost, the Lord-Veritants were, like the witch hunters of the Order of Azyr, tasked with rooting out spiritual and physical corruption – though in a far more direct manner than their mortal counterparts.

'I am simply ill at ease with such skulduggery, my friend,' Carus said. 'This is not the way it should be done. We should confront them openly, and drive back their shadows with our light.'

Carus thumped the ground with his staff, and the Lantern of Abjuration which surmounted it flashed softly.

'There will be plenty of that before the end, I have no doubt,' replied Gage. 'For now, we must meet shadow with shadow, lest our quarry take flight.'

'Yes.'

'Because they have an airship,' Gage added, after a moment.

'I understand.'

'Are you smiling? I can't tell.'

Carus grunted in noncommittal fashion, and Gage sighed. Trying to elicit a chuckle from his stolid companion had become something of a challenge for him. The Stormcast Eternal whistled sharply. The gryph-hound trotted towards him, carrying the remains of the rat in her beak, and Carus stroked the creature's wedge-shaped head affectionately.

'Good girl, Zephyr,' he rumbled.

Gage turned his attentions to the warehouse the dock-warden had indicated. Like most of the warehouses on the aether-dock, it was a square structure, built for durability rather than for looks. It followed the duardin design, with a high-peaked roof of flat planks that kept off the worst of the weather, and a shell of walkways and loading platforms that entrapped it. It seemed to crouch in the shadow of taller warehouses, a web of wooden gantries and skycutter berths stretching above it. A large aether-quay had been built onto the roof, projecting outwards like a semi-circular awning of wooden planks and support pillars.

Tarn's airship, the *Hopeful Traveller*, was docked there, floating above the city, snug in its nest of gangplanks, ropes and pulleys. It resembled a seagoing galley, save that its masts were burdened with thick canvas aether-bags rather than billowing sails. The double rows of oars on either side of the vessel were wide, fan-shaped assemblages of wood and cloth, perfect for catching the wind.

'The ship is still docked,' Gage murmured. 'Are you in there, I wonder?'

'Your spies say he is,' Carus said. Gage could almost hear the Stormcast frowning.

'Spies can be wrong. Or suborned.'

'We will find out soon enough. Whether he is or not, Rollo Tarn must be put to the question. And if he has committed crimes, he must be made to answer for them.'

Gage nodded absently. Rollo Tarn. The name was common enough, as was the man it was attached to. A human sky-merchant of some minor standing. While the Kharadron jealously guarded their routes through the skies of the Mortal Realms, a few daring individuals had learned of other paths, sailing more dangerous winds than those taken by the sky-duardin.

Now, thousands of airships, skycutters and leaf-boats found their way to the aether-docks every day, sailing along the rift-lanes. While they could fly neither as high nor as swiftly as the Kharadron vessels, they served much the same purpose, carrying goods between the two halves of the Twin-tailed City. It was mostly food, these days, but some, like Tarn, had become wealthy trading in building materials.

Despite the nature of the realm, coming by useable wood was difficult in Ghyran. The forests, by and large, belonged to the Everqueen and the sylvaneth tree-kin. Alarielle was the Goddess of Life, and Ghyran had been her demesne for as long as the Mortal Realms had existed. Though the Plague God, Nurgle, had all but wrested the realm from her, still she claimed a proprietary interest in it – the forests were hers, from the smallest sapling to the mightiest oak. And her servants would not hesitate to punish those who violated the ancient laws of the Everqueen, whatever their reasons.

Thus, logging was all but unheard of without great ritual and expense. Yet Tarn seemed to have no trouble bringing in copious amounts of timber, which the city's rulers, the Grand Conclave, bought eagerly, without asking too many questions. The city was hungry, in the way of all cities, and was expanding as its population swelled. Growing, as the God-King had decreed that it must. Such expansion was key to the eventual reconquest of the Mortal Realms, but it meant that the need for wood and stone was endless.

And Tarn was only too eager to supply it. The *Hopeful Traveller* brought in a new load of freshly cut timber every week, and it soon vanished into the city, to be made into new buildings and palisades. But where was the wood coming from? Not a whisper of Tarn's source had reached the usual gossips among the trade guilds. That, by itself, was suspicious.

Unfortunately, as far as the Grand Conclave was concerned, suspicion was not enough to cancel such a lucrative contract. Tarn had made himself integral to the city's growth. Not a crime, in itself, but there was something there. Gage could feel it.

'What seems perfect, rarely is,' he said softly.

It was a saying among his brethren in the order. Perfection was a mask worn by Chaos, and the prettiest faces often hid a singular ugliness beneath. It was his task to seek out that ugliness, and to purge it. Such was the duty handed down to the Order of Azyr and its servants by the God-King: to find the darkness, wherever it laired, and bring it to the light.

Instinctively, Gage ran a finger along the badge pinned to his lapel. The hammer and the comet. The sign of Sigmar Heldenhammer, God-King of Azyr. The founder of Azyrheim, and the creator of the Stormcast Eternals. It was Sigmar who had led the first tribes of mortal men out of barbarism and set them on the path of civilisation. And it was Sigmar who had freed the other gods from their ancient prisons, so that the Mortal Realms might flourish beneath their guidance.

It had been Sigmar who had first struck a blow against the Ruinous Powers, keeping the realms safe from their corrupting influence. And it would be Sigmar and his servants who would drive the Dark Gods back again, freeing the Mortal Realms from their monstrous clutches.

Sigmar was the light in the darkness, and that darkness was here. Not just in the city, but close by. Gage could smell it. Taste it. It was on the air, and in the water. It was like an itch he couldn't scratch. He realised he was tapping the pommel of his sword hard enough to make it rattle in its sheath. With an effort of will, he stopped himself. He felt Carus' eyes on him.

'You can feel it,' the Lord-Veritant rumbled. 'The call of Chaos.' He pressed a hand to his chest-plate. 'In here. Like the echo of a song you do not recall hearing. Or the whisper of an unfamiliar voice, echoing up out of the deep.'

Gage nodded. 'It seems impossible. To find it here, in a place sanctified by the hand of the God-King himself, and yet…'

'Sanctity is not enough. Even the strongest stones eventually crumble.'

'Yes.' Gage frowned. 'Tarn has friends in high places. They will not abandon him, not without proof. So we must find it, even if they would rather that we didn't.'

'Hammerhal is the greatest of the Cities of Sigmar, save Azyrheim itself. Anything that threatens it must be rooted out and brought to light. That is our task and our privilege.' Carus' voice was hard and sharp. 'None may gainsay us.'

'Not successfully, at any rate,' Gage murmured. Carus' gryphhound stiffened, the feathers on her neck ruffling. The Stormcast placed a restraining hand on her.

'Quietly, Zephyr,' he murmured. He glanced at Gage, and gestured upwards with his staff. 'Kuva is back.'

Gage looked up at the web of walkways and gantries above. A slim shape dropped down through them, landing lightly on the ground nearby. Despite the heavy fur cloak and armour she wore, she made no sound at all.

'Well?' Gage asked, as the newcomer rose to her feet.

He'd tasked Kuva with seeing to the rest of the dock-wardens on duty. He didn't want any interruptions or surprises, whatever the night brought. If Tarn knew he was being investigated, things would become that much more difficult.

'They will not trouble us,' Kuva said. The aelf's voice was a harsh rasp, and her fine-boned features were stern and marked by faint scars. The Lion Ranger was tall, taller than Gage, though still falling short of the towering Carus. She wore a long coat of golden scale mail beneath a cloak of white fur. Her flaxen hair was tied back from her face, revealing the tapered knife-points of her ears, and she rested a broad-bladed war-axe in the crook of her arm.

That axe, with its wide double blade, had tasted the blood of monsters and men alike, and she had wielded it for longer than Gage had been alive – perhaps even longer than the Mortal Realms themselves had existed. There were scribes who claimed that the origins of the Lion Rangers might stretch back to the world-that-was, but only Sigmar and his fellow gods knew for sure, and they weren't saying.

Some among his order whispered that Kuva had been there the day the last Gate of Azyr had slammed shut, sealing the Celestial Realm away from the rest of the Mortal Realms as they reeled beneath the assaults of Chaos. They also said that she had been there, waiting, the day it opened once more, centuries later. He could believe it.

'Dead?' Gage asked. Kuva was the type to cut a knot, rather than untie it.

'Unconscious. I do not kill slaves.'

Gage snorted. 'Hardly slaves. They're paid a fair wage.' He paused. 'Perhaps not enough to deal with the likes of us, but still. Comets in their pockets, and a roof over their heads. What more can any man ask?'

'Not to get hit on the head and hidden in a rubbish heap,' Bryn growled as he stepped out of the alleyway, dusting his hands. The duardin was almost as broad as Kuva was tall, and thick with muscle beneath the heavy gromril war-plate he wore. His bald dome of a head surmounted a thick profusion of greying beard, much of it bound in thick plaits. Beneath shaggy brows, two pale blue eyes twinkled with amusement. He wore a brace of drakefire pistols holstered across his barrel chest, and had a heavy two-handed hammer slung over his back.

'Then again, you humans are odds ones. Complaining about every little thing.' Bryn nodded back towards the alley. 'I hid him well.'

'Took you long enough,' Gage said.

'Don't ask, unless you want it done properly.'

Bryn had once served as an Ironbreaker in the retinue of a duardin warden king, though which one he had never said, just as he had never explained why he had left the king's service in the first place. The forge-proven armour he wore was decorated with golden knotwork and marked with Khazalid runes, which shone strangely in the light of Carus' staff.

Gage had worked with Kuva and Bryn for longer than he cared to calculate. A man in his profession needed trustworthy swords at his back, whatever their race. They may have had their own reasons for aiding him in his investigations, but they had saved his life – and he, theirs – more times than he could count.

By comparison, Carus was a newcomer, though the Stormcast Eternals of the Hallowed Knights had warded Hammerhal Ghyra since its founding. As a Lord-Veritant, Carus' authority exceeded Gage's own. While a Lord-Veritant's place was usually on the battlefield, they would occasionally aid the Order of Azyr if the need arose. In those instances, it was traditional that they defer to the order, though that often depended on the Lord-Veritant in question. Carus, for his part, seemed content to follow Gage's lead – at least for the moment.

Gage looked at the aelf. 'The warehouse?'

'Unguarded,' Kuva said. She hesitated. 'Or so it seems.'

'That's all to the good. If we can do this quietly, so much the better. We'll check the warehouse first, then the airship.'

'We should burn it,' the aelf added.

'Which – the warehouse, or the airship?'

'All of it.' She looked around with an expression of distaste.

Gage smiled. The Lion Ranger had little liking for cities, even one as beautiful as this. Her order were as much creatures of the wild as the beasts whose skins they wore. They were savage and graceful, with little tolerance for what they saw as the foibles of human- and duardin-kind. Especially when it came to the reliability – or the lack thereof – of walls and cities.

'I shall bear your suggestion in mind,' Gage said.

He tapped the grip of one of his pistols. The baroque weapons had been crafted in Azyrheim, long before Gage had been gifted them by his mentor upon his ascension to a full knight of the order. They were filled with blessed shot, and he had used them to end the life of more than one enemy of the Celestial Realm.

Bryn chuckled, a query mark of sweet smoke rising from the bowl of his pipe. He sniffed. 'Airships. Only a manling would think of such things.'

Gage glanced at him. 'Your cousins, the Kharadron, might beg to differ.'

'Aethercraft. Different sort of thing entirely. Duardin engineering, that. Not entirely respectable, but you have to make allowances sometimes.' He pointed at the airship. 'That, however, is a boat with a bag of hot air attached to it.' He puffed on his pipe. 'Might as well be magic.'

'It *is* magic,' Kuva said, looking down at the duardin. The aelf hefted her broad-bladed war-axe onto one shoulder. She frowned. 'Human magic.'

'Better than aelf magic, I suppose.'

'Quiet, Bryn,' Gage said firmly. 'I'm not concerned with how it flies, so much as what it might be carrying. And the sooner we check the warehouse, the sooner we find out. Let's go.'

Bryn gave a gap-toothed smile. 'Finally,' he said, before tapping out his pipe and stowing it somewhere in his armour.

Kuva led the way, moving quietly. Gage and Bryn followed close behind. Carus brought up the rear, moving more slowly, so as to reduce the clatter of his war-plate. Blessed sigmarite was many things, but mystically silent wasn't one of them.

A blow from Bryn's hammer was sufficient to shatter the lock on the warehouse doors. Kuva went in first. Gage followed, one hand on the hilt of his sword.

The warehouse spread out around him. The interior was high and vaulted, the upper reaches criss-crossed with walkways. Moss-lanterns hung from the floor-to-ceiling support beams, and the bioluminescent foxfire within them cast a pale glow across the source of Tarn's fortune: stacks of freshly cut logs.

The stacks were twice Gage's height, and made up of dozens of logs resting on heavy pallets. They filled the warehouse, front to back. The smell of green wood and pulp was thick on the air. And something else. Something indefinable. Gage looked around, frowning. Carus met his gaze, and nodded. He could sense it as well.

Gage had learned, through hard experience, to trust his instincts. There was something here. They just had to find it.

'Spread out,' he said softly, 'but stay in sight of one another.'

'What are we looking for?' Bryn said. The duardin studied the stacks warily.

'Anything suspicious.'

'More suspicious than two manlings, an aelf and a duardin sneaking around a warehouse in the middle of the night? The aelf's right. Let's just save time and burn it down.'

Gage looked at the duardin. It was an old game, this. The Dispossessed, those ancient duardin clans who'd lost their ancestral holds and lands, had little patience where Chaos was concerned. Concepts like guilt and innocence were inconsequential when it came to the very real threat of corruption. Many among the Order of Azyr shared that outlook. Gage did not. Every innocent condemned to the pyre only made the enemy's cause stronger.

When he didn't reply, Bryn chuckled. 'Aye, then, I guess not. I'll keep my eyes open.' He strode off, whistling softly.

Gage shook his head. If he and the others hadn't been working together as long as they had, he might have been worried.

He moved through the stacks carefully, studying them. Shadows cascaded across them in the soft glow of the moss-lanterns. More than once, he caught himself staring at a point in the darkness, thinking he'd seen something. But there was nothing there. He glanced over at Carus and his gryph-hound. The beast stalked about, hackles stiff and tail lashing. She sensed something.

'That makes two of us,' Gage muttered. He turned, fingers tapping against the pommel of his sword. It felt as if the warehouse were holding its breath somehow. As if something was watching… *waiting*. But what?

Gage turned. Some instinct, honed by years of investigation into dark places, drew him to the nearest stack of logs.

'Something about this wood,' he said to himself.

He pulled off his glove and ran his hand along the rough-hewn logs. The wood was dark, and sticky with sap. But it was sturdy, and good for building – surprisingly so, according to some of his sources. Where was Tarn getting it?

The bark seemed to wriggle beneath his touch, and he jerked his hand back.

'Sun and moon,' he muttered as the bark split, rearranging itself into the approximation of a grinning face. Sap ran down from the sides of its too-wide mouth like drool as it smacked its lips at him. An inhuman chuckle rose from the wood. The bark splintered and bulged, thinning like wet dough, as the face rose. Two massive pink hands squirmed out of a knothole that was far too small to contain them. They clutched at Gage, and he stumbled back.

'Carus!'

'Avaunt, filth!' the Lord-Veritant roared from behind him.

He struck the floor with the ferrule of his staff, and the Lantern of Abjuration atop it blazed brightly. Azure light washed over the stacks of wood. The thing in front of Gage squealed and retreated into its log, diminishing like smoke being drawn through a flue. As the light faded, Gage heard the scuff of bare feet on the floor. He spun, drawing his rapier.

'Ambush!' he cried.

He blocked a blow meant to stave in his skull, and opened his attacker's throat with a quick slash. He looked down at the man he had killed. He was muscular and clad in dark robes, his head hidden behind a golden mask and his hand still limply clutching a serrated blade. The mask leered up at him, vaguely avian, but horribly, hideously something else. Gage felt a chill course through him at the sight of the ruinous sigils etched onto the mask. They seemed to twist in on themselves in the dim glow of the moss-lanterns.

'The Changer of Ways,' he hissed.

It was the mark of Tzeentch – the Chaos God of deception and fortune. Its acolytes came in secret, wearing the mask of innocence. While the servants of the other Dark Gods haunted the fringes of civilisation, the servants of Tzeentch nestled within it like a black seed. They could be anyone and anything.

His suspicions regarding Tarn were true then. Gage felt no triumph, only a sick sensation as he gazed at the stacks of wood. Shadows clumped across the logs in strange patterns, and he felt a chill as a sound like thousands of rats scuttling across the stacks whispered through the warehouse.

Daemons. There were daemons in the wood.

The thought of such hell-born nightmares loose in the world was repulsive to him on a spiritual level. Daemons were shards of the Dark Gods made hideous flesh. They could only be called forth into the material realm by certain abominable rites, practised by those who had given themselves over body and soul to the Ruinous Powers.

Laughter echoed through the warehouse. The moss-lanterns flickered and went out, plunging the building into darkness. Gage could hear the rustle of cloth and the thump of feet. More acolytes? Or something worse?

'Guard yourselves – we are not alone in here.' He drew a pistol.

'No, you most certainly are not… Gage, is it?' a voice called out. It seemed to echo from nowhere and everywhere. Instinctively, Gage looked up, but he could see no one on the shadowed walkways above. 'A knight of the Order of Azyr,' the speaker continued. 'I would be flattered, if your sort were not thick as fleas in the cities of men. It was inevitable that one of you would pull on the thread of fate and come for us.'

'Us? Us who? Who are you? Tarn?' Gage spoke loudly. Sometimes the servants of the Dark Gods liked to talk. That volubility could be used against them. At the very least, it might buy him some time. Motes of ugly light danced across the stacks of wood, and Gage thought he could make out more daemonic faces squirming in the bark. The air took on an oily tang.

He glanced up and spotted a shape he thought was Kuva creeping along the top of a nearby stack of wood. How the aelf had gotten up there so quickly, he couldn't say. But he knew she was searching for the source of the laughter. He needed to buy her time to do so.

'Well?' he continued. 'Whom do I have the honour of addressing?'

More laughter, though it wasn't the wild cackle of a lunatic, which only made it worse. As it faded, voices rose in a slow, sonorous chant. The moss-lanterns blazed to new life, revealing dozens of men and women, wearing golden masks and standing in ragged rows between the stacks. The acolytes of Tzeentch were clad much like the man he'd killed, and they were clutching a variety of weapons. Without the masks and robes, they could have been anyone: merchants, farmers, sewerjacks or beggars.

'Bryn? Carus? I could use some help,' Gage called out, hoping they would reach him before the acolytes overwhelmed him.

'Who are we?' the voice called out. 'We are your neighbours, witch hunter. We are the devoted, singing false praises to the tyrant-god, Sigmar. We are the labourers who work so hard in the orchards and fields, harvesting the bounty of Ghyran to feed those who live on the other side of the realmgate. We are you.'

'Always so theatrical,' Gage said, and fired.

A mask pitched backwards. The chanting ceased, and the acolytes came at him in a rush. He met the first of them with his rapier, but there were too many to face alone. For every one he downed, two more took his or her place. The acolytes did not scream as they came, but instead chanted. It might have been a word, or perhaps a name. The sound of it grated against Gage's ears and pricked at his concentration. It was all he could do to keep their blades from finding him.

'Gage – look out!' Kuva shouted from somewhere above him.

He glanced up, and saw Kuva dart across the top of a stack, moving swiftly. As she ran, she sliced through the ropes holding the stack together. Logs rumbled down, smashing into the surprised acolytes. The aelf rode the rolling logs to the bottom of the stack and leapt. She landed among a knot of acolytes. Her war-axe flashed, and bodies fell.

'Quick thinking,' Gage shouted appreciatively.

She glanced at him, and nodded. Then her eyes widened, and Gage felt a tremor run through the boards beneath his feet. He whirled, almost too late, and dodged aside. A heavy spiked flail crashed down, pulping several of the logs. He scrambled back.

The flail's wielder was no man in a mask. Instead, it was a being out of nightmare – a hulking brute, clad in turquoise armour. One half of its chest and one arm were bare of armour, revealing pale flesh, surmounted by a monstrous growth – a twisted, parasitic sibling, eyeless and chattering, its thin arms clutching a staff. The brute drew the sword slung from its hip with its free hand, a sickly flame clinging to the blade.

Gage stared at it in horror. 'Curseling,' he whispered.

He'd read of such monsters, and heard stories from other members of his order. Curselings had once been men, before their lust for secret knowledge had twisted them into silent repositories of foul lore. The growth on its shoulder was a tretchlet, a daemonic homunculus – a physical manifestation of all that the curseling had learned.

The eyeless tretchlet gibbered in excitement and slashed the air with its staff, as if urging its hulking sibling on. The curseling's breath rasped like a bellows, gusting from the vents in its featureless helm. It swung the flail again, splintering a log and showering Gage with shards of bark. He ducked back. He couldn't match its strength.

He glanced around, seeking aid, but it looked as if his companions were preoccupied. Kuva was surrounded by a ring of acolyte blades. He could hear Carus bellowing nearby, and the shriek of his gryph-hound. And Bryn...

'*Khazukan Khazuk-ha!*' Bryn roared as he crashed into the curseling, knocking it back a step. The duardin spun his hammer about as if it weighed less than nothing, striking again and again. Bryn glanced at Gage. 'You called, I came, manling.' He hit the curseling again, staggering it.

With a snarl, it slashed at him, the burning blade carving greasy contrails through the air before it chopped into the floor. The duardin avoided the blow and drove the ferrule of his hammer into the side of the creature's skull. The curseling moaned and caught Bryn a glancing blow with its flail, sending the duardin skidding across the warehouse floor, scattering acolytes.

The creature spun away from the dazed duardin, moving

quicker than Gage had expected. The vile, blue-green radiance of its baroque war-plate stung his eyes, and he fell back before its onslaught. The flail it wielded in one hand slammed down, shattering the wooden planks of the floor. A moment later, its sword hissed out, trailing unnatural flames. Gage retreated, trying to put some distance between them.

Beyond the curseling, he could see Kuva fighting her way towards Bryn, who was clambering slowly to his feet. Acolytes crouched on the walkways above chanted and gestured, unleashing crackling bolts of sorcerous energy. The aelf dived aside, narrowly avoiding the explosive darts. She leapt over the cursing duardin, and lightly scrambled up the stack of logs, her eyes fixed on the walkways above.

He lost sight of his companions as the curseling's flail snapped out again, nearly taking his head off. He ducked aside and drew a thin line of ichor from its bare arm with the tip of his rapier. The monstrous tretchlet undulated towards him, its eyeless face contorted in a snarl. It swung its staff at his head, gibbering in rage.

A long blade interposed itself, catching the blow. Carus forced the curseling back a step, as staff and sword screeched apart in a scattering of sparks.

'No, beast, face me,' the Stormcast rumbled. 'I am Sigmar's light, and his wrath, made manifest. I am the faithful.'

The curseling groaned in wordless anticipation and stomped towards this new foe. Gage took the opportunity to draw the second of his pistols. He took aim at the curseling's broad back as it traded thunderous blows with the Lord-Veritant – the two massive warriors seemed evenly matched, but Gage had no intention of leaving things to chance.

The curseling was only a slave – a tool of the cult. Its master, the cult's magister, would be close by, watching the fray through the eyes of the curseling itself. The magister was Tarn. It had to be.

But the question was – where was he? Gage pushed the thought aside. Time enough for that later. He took a steadying breath and squeezed the trigger.

The boom of the pistol was loud, but the curseling's scream was even louder. It convulsed in agony and spun. It lunged, and its burning blade nearly opened Gage from crown to crotch. The tretchlet spat something in a shrill voice, and a sorcerous bolt erupted from the homunculus' twitching hands. Gage swung behind a support pillar. Heat enveloped him as the bolt struck it. He could smell fire, and realised that the warehouse had been set aflame.

The curseling's blade chopped into the pillar, just above his head. Gage shoved away from it and slashed at the brute. It groaned and struck at him with its flail. An acolyte lunged at Gage, blade slashing a button from his coat. He spitted the cultist, all too aware of the curseling looming over him, blade raised. He turned and looked up into the creature's empty gaze. There was no malice there, no hatred – only passionless intent. It was an automaton of meat, hollowed out and repurposed by forces beyond the ken of man. It raised its blade, and the flames limning its brutal length blazed with hideous radiance.

With a howl, Zephyr leapt atop it. The gryph-hound savaged the tretchlet with her beak as she clung to the brute's shoulder. The curseling warbled in rage and began to thrash, trying to dislodge the tenacious beast. Gage saw his chance and lunged, driving his blade home into the creature's unprotected armpit. His sword grated on bone and then sunk past, into something soft. Something important, he hoped.

The curseling stiffened, twin screams echoing from both heads. It staggered back, pulling itself off Gage's blade. With a convulsive heave, it hurled the gryph-hound away before turning and lumbering off into the darkness, leaving a trail of ichor in its wake.

Gage took a step after it. It would take more than that to kill such a beast. Several acolytes moved to block his path. They raised their hands, chanting, conjuring sorcerous bolts. He tensed as the searing bursts of magical energy hurtled towards him, too close to dodge. Suddenly, Carus stepped between Gage and the sorcerous missiles. He swept out his staff, and the shimmering bolts dissipated in the light of the Lantern of Abjuration.

From above, he heard a scream, and stepped back as the body of an acolyte crashed to the floor. He looked up and saw Kuva on the walkway, war-axe dark with the blood of her foes. The aelf looked down and gestured with her head.

'Gage – go! The duardin and I are more than capable of killing a few fools in bird masks.'

Gage hesitated, but only for a moment. She was right. He caught Carus' eye and gestured. The Lord-Veritant nodded solemnly and whistled. His gryph-hound gave a squalling bark and loped in pursuit of the fleeing curseling. The nimble beast would stay on its trail, whatever obstacle lay between them.

Carus started after the creature, his tread shaking the floor-boards. His staff snapped out to club one acolyte from his feet, even as his sword slashed down to crack another's shield in two. Gage hurried in his wake, reloading his pistol as he ran.

'Come, witch hunter,' Carus growled. 'Our quarry seeks the safety of the shadows. Let us drag him into the light!'

CHAPTER THREE

THE STEEL SOULS

Serena Sunstrike, Liberator of the Steel Souls Warrior Chamber, caught the first blow on her shield. Guided by instincts honed on the training fields of the Gladitorium, the Hallowed Knights warrior swept a second slash aside with her warblade. Undaunted, her attacker lunged, pressing its assault with a savage ferocity. She met it, matching her mystically enhanced prowess against its unnatural strength.

The beast before her might have been a man once. Now it was a twisted thing, avian-like, with curling horns and a curved, stabbing beak. Its blue flesh was marked by intricate tattoos and ruinous sigils, and its bronze armour stank of unnatural oils. It leapt forwards, yelping and gibbering, a serrated blade in either hand, trying to force her back.

All around her, the Hexwood echoed with the clamour of battle. Silver-and-azure-clad Hallowed Knights, alongside mortal Freeguild warriors wearing the white-and-blue uniforms of the Faithful Blades regiment, fought against the savage tzaangors that sought to overwhelm their lines. The creatures were devoted servants of Tzeentch, serving their dark god with bestial cunning and fierce strength.

Her opponent brought both its blades down on the rim of her shield, jerking her off balance. It darted forwards, the hook of its beak scraping against her war-mask. Instinctively, she snapped her head forwards to meet it. Silver sigmarite crunched against malformed bone, and the beast reeled with a squawk. Before it could recover, she sank the edge of her warblade into its skull.

The tzaangor collapsed, but there were others to take its place – more of its kind loped out from the trees, their trilling shrieks pounding upon the air as they crashed into the Stormcasts' shieldwall.

'They're trying to overwhelm us,' the warrior beside Serena snarled, stamping forwards. His warblade chopped down into his foe's skull.

'I have eyes, Ravius,' Serena replied.

The attack was as savage as it had been sudden. One moment, the forest had been silent. Then, strange twittering calls had echoed through the trees, accompanied by the sound of pine needles crunching beneath many feet, before the first of the beastkin had burst from the dark corridors of shadow between the scaly trunks of the looming pine trees. They came accompanied by the frenetic clamour of unseen musicians – wild horns skirled, and great drums thumped, somewhere deep in the forest.

That the Hallowed Knights and their mortal allies had been seeking the very creatures who now assaulted them did not make Serena feel better about the situation. The intent had been to crush the creatures in their lair, but the column of Stormcast Eternal and Freeguild warriors had been caught all but unawares by the ambush, and now fought by lantern light.

Unlike the towering Stormcasts, the soldiery of the Freeguild were naught but mortals. But what they lacked in size and strength, they made up for in the discipline with which they faced the enemy. The

Faithful Blades fought as they had been trained to fight, leveraging halberd, crossbow and handgun against their bestial enemies.

Stormcast Judicators and Freeguild crossbowmen loosed volley after volley from their positions by the supply wagons as the beastkin raced into the light. Freeguild warriors thrust halberds between the shoulders of the Stormcasts and over the rims of their locked shields, forming an uncompromising bulwark – at least for the moment.

Serena flinched as a crackle of azure lightning signalled the death of a fellow Stormcast Eternal. The lightning surged upwards with a deafening snarl and punched through the thick canopy, streaking into the dark green of the sky.

'Another soul gone home to Azyr,' Ravius said, shoving his opponent back.

The tzaangor staggered, screeching. Serena opened its throat with a quick slash and silenced it.

'May they find themselves forged anew, stronger than before,' she said. She turned, avoiding a blow, and responded in kind. She blinked away the afterimage of the lightning flash, trying to clear her vision as another of the twisted beastkin bounded towards her, shrieking out guttural war cries.

She wheeled to meet it, her pulse thundering in her ears. She drove the rim of her shield into the throat of the beast as it reached her, and it collapsed in a choking heap, dropping its weapons. She ran it through before it could rise. It clawed at her forearm as she twisted the blade, stilling its heart.

Light blazed forth suddenly, filling the glade and driving back the shadows. Serena turned, knowing the source of the radiance even as she did so. Lord-Celestant Gardus, the Steel Soul himself, fought at the centre of the battle-line, wielding a runeblade in one hand and a hammer in the other. His form blazed with a holy light – it seeped between the joins in his silver aegis war-plate, and grew brighter with every passing moment.

The beastkin confronting him fell back, their unnatural flesh steaming. They staggered as if blinded and stumbled away, seeking the safety of the dark. The heavily armoured Paladin Retributors surrounding Gardus caught them before they got far, their crackling lightning hammers slamming down on the beastkin.

The Paladin cohort, clad in thick bastion armour and wielding massive two-handed lightning hammers, were often found wherever the fighting was the thickest. At their head was Feros of the Heavy Hand, a great roaring giant of a warrior. Feros wielded his hammer with a startling elegance, and shouted imprecations at the enemy as he smashed them aside. Twisted bones snapped and splintered, and the creatures fell, their wails of pain silenced moments later.

Gardus' light swelled as he pressed the counter-attack, he and his bodyguards driving the creatures before them with brutal efficiency. Some said the light was a blessing from Sigmar – a sign of both Gardus' faith and the God-King's favour. Others, less charitably, murmured that it was a sign that something had changed in the Steel Soul – that he was both less and more than the man he had been, before he had fallen in battle with the forces of Chaos.

Duty did not end with death for a Stormcast Eternal. To fall in battle was to be reforged on the Anvil of Apotheosis, to have the broken shards of one's body and soul hammered once more into useful shape. Serena had not yet endured a second Reforging, but she had heard the stories from those who had suffered such a fate: the rush of celestial lightning, the impossible agony of rebirth… and worst of all, the loss that came with such a renewal. More and more of the tenuous memories of who they had been were stripped away with every death, reducing Stormcast warriors to taciturn automatons.

The thought of that loss, more than any other, unsettled her. What were they without memory? Without that tether to mortal existence, what was left of them? Already she could not recall much about who she had been before. It was as if those memories belonged to a different person; they crowded at the edges of her mind.

She shook the nagging thoughts aside and raised her shield, the flat of her blade balanced on the rim. Around her, the shieldwall reformed as the beasts fell back from Gardus' light. She could hear Aetius, the Liberator-Prime of her cohort, bellowing orders.

'Lock shields – lock them, I said! Reform the line!'

Known as the Shieldborn, Aetius was a stolid sort, stubborn and determined. He stalked behind the battle-line, his silver armour tarnished, his hammer encrusted with gore.

'They're running,' Ravius said excitedly. He took a step forwards, as if to pursue, and Serena almost joined him, caught up in his eagerness. The battle-line wavered on the cusp of pursuit. 'We can finish them!'

'Don't be foolish – haring off after them only earns a useless death and weakens our lines,' Aetius snapped. 'Are you new-forged? Remember your training.' He caught hold of Serena. 'Lock shields, I said.'

'This is not my first battle,' Serena said, stung. She shook him off.

'Yes, but the Gladitorium is different, isn't it?' he chided. 'More like play than war, though blood is spilled all the same. This is the real thing.' Aetius studied her. His gaze was unwavering, and she met it without flinching.

'I am faithful,' she said.

Aetius nodded.

'Good enough.' He dropped a heavy fist on her shoulder. 'Hold position, sister, until I say otherwise. That goes for all of you – hold, until I say.' His voice rolled down the line, made unnaturally loud by Sigmar's gifts. He slammed his hammer against his shield. 'Who will stand, though the shadows lengthen?'

'Only the faithful!' Serena and the others shouted in reply.

They struck their shields with their weapons, whether warblade or hammer, casting the sound after their fleeing foes like a roll of thunder. The beasts ran, shrieking and heedless. The sound of their fading cries ratcheted through her, pricking at her consciousness.

It all seemed familiar, somehow, as if she had heard that same sound long ago. But she could not recall the circumstances. It wasn't the first time – she often heard the murmur of familiar voices, but could not tell what they said, or to whom they belonged. Even worse, she sometimes saw faces in her mind's eye – achingly familiar, yet she could put no name to them, no matter how she tried.

Frustrated, she struck her shield again.

She was not alone in this affliction of memory. All Stormcasts suffered from it to a greater or lesser degree. Those reforged earliest remembered the most about their mortal existence, while those crafted in the Second or Third Striking remembered less, as if the process were somehow being perfected.

Those few memories she had were invariably painful. She knew that those whose faces and voices haunted her were now long since dust, their souls gone down to the dreamless lands of the dead. All that she had been, all that she might have become, was lost.

No – not lost. *Sacrificed.* Forged anew on the Anvil of Apotheosis, made into something stronger and better. Something that could stand between the innocent and the darkness which threatened to consume them all.

All that mattered was who she was now: Serena Sunstrike, Liberator of the Shieldborn conclave, and a Hallowed Knight of the Steel Souls Warrior Chamber. This would have to be enough. Perhaps later, when the war was finished, she might be allowed to be something else. She shook herself, pushing the thought aside. There was enough to worry about without thinking of a future that might never be.

It had been almost a century since Sigmar had reopened the Gates of Azyr and cast the storm of his wrath into the Mortal Realms. Almost a century since the first Stormcast Eternals had hurled back the servants of the Dark Gods and established their beachheads in the realms of Fire, Metal, Beasts and Life.

Serena had witnessed some of these battles first-hand. She had fought alongside her conclave as they strove to claim the ancient realmgate known as the Gates of Dawn. She had seen the resurrection of the Everqueen at the Blackstone Summit, and watched as Alarielle's divine fury drove back the forces of Nurgle at the Genesis Gate during the All-Gates War.

And now, in the wake of those first bloody engagements, a new age had begun. Armies of men, duardin and aelves had marched forth from Azyr to retake ancestral lands long since lost to Chaos, or to build new homes in unfamiliar realms. New cities rose on the bones of the old, and ancient alliances were renewed.

She heard the rattle of Azyrite drums, and glanced back. Within the safety of the Stormcast shieldwall, the mortal soldiers of the Freeguild moved swiftly, fortifying the glen with practiced alacrity. Such measures had become second nature to them: Ghyran was neither tame nor safe, for all that the Everqueen had made common cause with the God-King against their common foes. The forests of the Realm of Life were savage places, even when they weren't occupied by packs of Chaos beasts.

They hadn't planned to make camp here. They hadn't planned to make camp at all – the forest was too dangerous for that – but with the enemy massing around them, there was no way to press on to the forest's heart, where the creatures supposedly laired, without incurring grievous losses. They had come to wipe the beastkin out and free the forest from their depredations, but that was easier said than done.

Serena looked around. The Hexwood sprawled across the

hardscrabble slopes of the Nevergreen Mountains which rose west of Hammerhal Ghyra. Scaly pine trees grew tall and strong, their roots coiling through the flaky soil and their wide branches all but blocking out the night sky. It was not a pleasant sort of forest. The dancing shadows gave the trees faces, and more than once she thought she saw something leering at her from the branches above.

The clearing the column occupied was large, but was still a thin spot in all the thick. The trees rose upwards or fell away at odd angles, following the incline of the slope. The Nevergreen Mountains were a broken jumble of crags, shrouded in scrub pines and thick underbrush – neither truly mountains nor hills, but something in between. The column led by the Hallowed Knights was strung out in a rough battle-line among the trees, but that line began to contract as the last yowls of the retreating tzaangors faded and temporary defensive emplacements were erected.

The clearing echoed with the sounds of labour as the Freeguilders completed their tasks. Stakes linked by stout chains were hammered into the hard soil around the edges of the clearing, their points jutting towards the dark trees. Supply wagons were circled, the lumbering ghyrochs which pulled them lowing in confusion as they were hauled about by their handlers. The massive beasts were covered in shaggy, moss-like hair, and their wide, flat heads bore impressive branch-like horns. Their stony hooves tore the soil in discontent as the ghyrochs scented blood.

Besides casks of fresh water, gunpowder and crates of shot, one of the supply wagons carried the *Impertinent Maiden* – an ancient helblaster volley gun. This lethal war-machine was an arrangement of stacked gun barrels connected to a sturdy framework. It was capable of unleashing a volley of shot at an approaching enemy, when it wasn't otherwise busy being jammed or blowing a gasket.

The gun's crew, in their blue-and-white livery, were fussing over the engine like concerned parents, though they hadn't had time to use it in the battle. The wagon bearing it was pulled into the centre of the defensive ring, so that the *Impertinent Maiden* could unleash her affections more effectively should the need arise.

And that need was likely. The tzaangors were gone, but only for the moment. The thud of their drums still sounded deep in the forest. Occasionally, Serena caught a flash of sickly light far back in the trees. She felt eyes on her, watching. Calculating.

Unsettled, she turned her attentions to the soldiers' efforts. The Faithful Blades regiment had fought alongside the Steel Souls since the first Azyrites had followed the Stormcasts to the battlegrounds of the Jade Kingdoms nearly thirty years before. The Freeguild regiment's uniform incorporated the heraldry of the Hallowed Knights, and they were among the most devout of the mortal soldiery of the armies of Azyr. For them, faith was as good as armour. A handful of warrior-priests, clad in blue robes and silver war-plate, moved among them, leading the soldiers in prayer as they worked, or else reading loudly from the *Canticles of War*.

While the regiment itself was currently garrisoned out of Fort Gardus, some units had been seconded to act as auxiliaries for the expedition into the Hexwood. The Hallowed Knights did not begrudge the presence of these mortal allies. A Thunderhead Brotherhood was more than a match for most things that walked or crawled, but the Stormcast Eternals did not know the terrain, and the Freeguilders did. They had been fighting beast-kin in these regions since the fort's construction. Serena smiled slightly. It had been named for the Steel Soul, though he seemed much embarrassed by the honour.

Fort Gardus was a mighty bastion of stone and wood on the border of the Scabrous Sprawl, within several days' march of Hammerhal Ghyra. While it had originally been raised to keep watch on the daemon-haunted wastes of the Sprawl, it had grown into the central node of a defensive network of smaller fortresses and watchtowers stretching from the western lowlands to the marshes of the Verdant Bay. Much like the Hallowed Knights themselves, it warded Hammerhal from the relentless dangers of Ghyran.

'Get those bodies out from underfoot,' a voice barked. 'Quickly now.'

Serena made room as several apologetic Freeguilders moved through the shieldwall, dragging a dead tzaangor out past the stakes. She glanced back and saw a familiar face.

Sergeant Ole Creel had gone grey in the Faithful Blade's service, and his shoulders were bowed with the weight of experience. But his hands were steady, and his blue-and-white uniform was clean. One leg was a wooden prosthesis. Coins had been nailed to its polished length, and they gleamed gold in the lantern light. He wore a sergeant's badge on his cap, and had the twin-tailed comet etched into his battered chest-plate.

Creel had fought beside the Steel Souls for most of his life. Serena could recall a younger Creel, with an unlined face and two good legs, fighting in the front lines. He had marched through foetid jungles and over blistered fields, singing the praises of the God-King. Even when he'd lost his leg, his faith had never wavered. And now, he was an old man, but still faithful. Still loyal.

He doffed his feathered cap as he realised she was looking.

'My lady,' he said respectfully. The mortal soldiers of Azyr regarded the Stormcasts with awe, when they did not worship them outright as the manifestation of the God-King's will.

'Sergeant Creel,' she said as she stepped back out of line.

Other Stormcast Eternals were doing the same, seeing to wounds or cleaning their weapons, though most remained where they were, facing outwards with a stolidity born of hard experience. Serena caught Aetius' eye, and he nodded tersely, allowing her the break in discipline.

'You are unhurt?' she asked Creel.

'All my remaining limbs accounted for. Knock on wood.' The sergeant rapped his knuckles against his wooden leg. He gave her a gap-toothed grin and settled his cap back on his head. 'Bit of a fight, that. Thought they might get past you there, for a second.'

She looked down at one of the dead beastkin. For a moment, she was struck by a curious sense of déjà vu. Had beasts like these been responsible for the death of the woman she had been? She did not think so, but the mind often played tricks where such things were concerned.

'Have you seen their like before?' she asked.

'Twist-beaks,' Creel said, almost spitting the word. 'We've fought them too often of late. They're getting bold, out here in the dark places. High time we purged them from these woods with fire and shot.' He nudged the dead beast with his wooden foot. 'Cunning beasts. Tricky.' He squinted at the surrounding trees, a speculative look on his face. 'Too tricky by half.' He straightened. 'They don't attack like this, not without some plan in mind.'

'Perhaps we startled them.'

Creel nodded absently. 'Could be. Or maybe they were here to delay us.'

'An ambush to set up an ambush?'

He glanced at her. 'I've seen it before. Tricky, like I said.' He watched his warriors work. 'Be easier if we could fell some trees. Clear some ground.'

'That would not be wise,' Serena said. 'This land is not ours.'

'Well, someone already has.' He gestured to a nearby stump. 'Sawed clean, some of these trees. My father was a logger in the Nordrath Mountains. I know whereof I speak.' Creel grimaced. 'Besides, back at Fort Gardus, they say the sylvaneth and their queen have taken a liking to the Steel Soul. That they have an accord with him, and that it is only through his grace that we are allowed to pass through these forests.' Creel washed his mouth out with a drink from his water skin, and spat. 'Otherwise they'd tear us apart as swiftly as they do the servants of Chaos.'

'You disapprove?' Serena said, somewhat amused.

The Freeguilder frowned. 'Can't trust the tree-kin. They change with the seasons – calm one moment, wrathful the next. Chop down the wrong tree, and suddenly you're up to your neck in brambles. Or worse.'

'The Lady of Leaves guards her places well,' one of the other Freeguilders said. She was a tall woman, and she wore a torc of wood around her neck. She touched it as she spoke. 'This realm is hers, and it is by her will that we are allowed to breathe its air.'

'Quiet, Shael,' Creel barked. He glanced apologetically at Serena. 'Ignore her, lady. She's a local. Never known the blessed light of Sigmar, these Verdians. Think the Everqueen will stoop to save them from the Ruinous Powers, when she can't even save herself.'

These days, the Faithful Blades included both native Verdians and expatriate Azyrites in its ranks. Most of the Freeguilds responsible for the defence of Hammerhal Ghyra did. Rates of attrition were high, as the Freeguild sought to impose some sense of order on the ancient routes which connected Verdia to the rest of the Jade Kingdoms. It was hard, bloody work, and on more days than not, the skies near Hammerhal Ghyra were thick with carrion birds and powder smoke.

While Nurgle's hold on Ghyran had been weakened, the corrupted servants of the Plague God still prowled the wilds in substantial numbers, and their raids on the bastions of Azyr continued unabated. The Lord of Pestilence had once held Ghyran entire in his rotting clutches, and he sought obsessively to reclaim that small portion which Sigmar and the Everqueen had wrested back from him.

'And why wouldn't she?' Shael countered. 'We kept faith with her, while your folk were hiding behind high walls and sealed gates.'

'Remember whose sigil you wear, Verdian,' Creel snapped, his weather-beaten features flushing with anger. 'Your folk wouldn't even be here, free of corruption, if it wasn't for us. We of Azyr paid a heavy price in blood and steel to buy back your lands from the Plague God.' He thumped his false leg for emphasis.

'And we would not have found ground worth defending, were it not for the Everqueen and all those who serve her, mortal or otherwise,' a deep voice rumbled. Instantly, the squabbling Freeguilders fell silent and bowed their heads.

Serena turned. 'Lord-Celestant Gardus,' she said in greeting.

Gardus Steel Soul towered over the mortals who accompanied him. They were local tribesfolk, impressed into service as guides. They wore furs and battered leather hauberks. Their faces were tattooed with the whorl leaf-shapes common to the mountain clans of the region. They carried bows of sinew and short-hafted axes, and looked as if they knew how to use both. They stared about nervously, intimidated by the Stormcast warriors clad in silver.

Like Serena, the Lord-Celestant was clad in silver-and-azure war-plate, though his was more ornate by far, as befitted his rank. His heavy runeblade was sheathed at his side, but he carried his tempestos hammer in one hand. The weapon, like the warrior who wielded it, glowed with a subdued radiance.

'You are one of Aetius' warriors.' It wasn't a question, but Serena nodded anyway. 'You saw the brunt of it just now, sister.' He looked at her, head tilted enquiringly.

'Sunstrike, my lord,' she said. Then, a moment later, she added, 'Serena.' She bowed slightly and Gardus chuckled. It was a deep sound, gentle but far-reaching. She was suddenly glad for her war-mask, which hid her flush of embarrassment.

'Serena, then.' He looked at Creel. 'And you are… Sergeant Creel, are you not? You took the enemy standard at the Pale Gorge.' Gardus glanced down. 'You lost your leg there.'

'Fair trade, my lord, all things considered.' Creel grinned. 'Sigmar smiled on us.'

'He did, and he still does.' Gardus looked at the Freeguilders. 'That such men and women as you stand here before me is proof enough of that.' He gestured to Serena. 'What do you see here, sister?'

'I…' She hesitated, suddenly uncertain.

Gardus took pity on her. He laid a hand on her shoulder, and looked at the Freeguilders. 'I see folk from Azyr, Ghyran and Aqshy, standing side by side. As it should be – to defend one realm is to defend eight. For if one should fall, the others will follow in time. Even holy Azyr cannot stand alone, not for long.' Gardus turned, scanning the trees. 'We fight in Sigmar's name. We are his tempest made manifest. And we cleanse the land for all people, whether they were born in Azyrheim or Verdia.'

His words carried across the clearing. Many of the Freeguilders had stopped to listen. That had no doubt been his intent, Serena realised. His words had been meant to quell the grumbling before it could get started. But that had not been their sole purpose. Gardus *believed*, and his faith was like a warm wind on their souls, easing the chill of the shadows that gathered about them.

As Creel and the others went back to work, Gardus leaned close. 'I apologise,' he said softly. 'I saw an opportunity and took it.'

'I understand, my lord.'

'Discontent can afflict even the most loyal heart.' A ghyroch bellowed, and Gardus watched as its handler tried to calm the mossy creature. The smell of blood, and perhaps of the forest itself, had disconcerted the beasts and they tossed their horns and pawed the ground in dismay. 'There are wounds not yet healed. If they are allowed to fester, all that we work towards will be for nothing.' He looked at her. 'Do you understand?'

'I… Yes.' She did. Though the armies of Azyr had spilled into the

Mortal Realms with the intent to throw back Chaos, not everyone appreciated the kind of aid they brought. For many in the Mortal Realms, the closing of the Gates of Azyr was a legendary betrayal.

The Azyrites could be full of their own righteousness, often to a burdensome degree. Some among them looked down on those they had come to save, or worse, thought them to be tainted by the very act of their survival in Chaos-held lands. She looked at the Lord-Celestant.

'Is it true we are here at the request of the sylvaneth, my lord?'

Gardus hesitated, and she wondered if she had spoken out of turn. But Gardus encouraged a certain informality among his warriors.

'We are,' he said. 'They did not ask openly, for that is not their way. Instead, they passed their warning through the foresters.' He gestured to the tribesfolk in their furs and skins. 'They brought word to us, in turn.' He looked up, studying the trees which rose around them. 'And the sylvaneth are here. Watching. Waiting to see if we are as good as our word.'

Serena tensed. She looked around, remembering the faces she'd thought she'd seen in the trees. The sylvaneth moved through forests as easily as she might walk across open ground. Could that have been them?

'Watching us?' she asked. 'Why?'

'Not us,' Gardus said. He looked at her. 'Some wounds are worse than others, Serena Sunstrike. And even the strongest warrior sometimes needs the help of another.'

His hand fell to the hilt of his runesword, and he stared at the trees. She wondered if he could sense something. She listened, but heard only the faint thump of the beastkin drums, deep in the woods and far away.

Gardus looked at the tribesmen. 'Isn't that right, Hyrn?'

'It is, Bright One,' the tribesman said gruffly. He was older than the rest, his greying mane held out of his face by a headband of leather. He spoke the Azyrite tongue well enough, though his accent was guttural. He caught her look and tapped his throat. 'The priests teach us. Say we must speak the star-tongue, or Sigmar will not hear us.'

'Faith needs no words,' Serena said. Hyrn smiled and nodded.

'Yes. The Lady of Leaves is always listening.' His smile faded. 'Though some feel that she does not do even that these days. We've seen witch-light flickering among the trees. It's said that the beastkin dance here now, where the forest spirits once did.' He frowned and spat. 'The beastkin drove them away, and made the air and ground sour. Soon, they will drive the last of us away as well. Or worse – we will join them in their dancing, as so many of our folk have.'

He shuddered, and Serena frowned, recalling what she had heard of the corrupting magics of Tzeentch. How many of his people had Hyrn seen twisted into monsters, warped body and soul by witchcraft he had no defence against?

Gardus laid a hand on the tribesman's shoulder. 'No more will join them – this I swear to you, by the light of Sigendil. That is why we are here. We will not abandon you.'

Serena made to reply, when she felt the wind shift. The smell of death was replaced by something even fouler. Creel and the other mortals nearby coughed as the sickly sweet scent wafted over them. Serena turned and raised her shield. She knew that scent – sorcery. Something was happening. The air had taken on a greasy pall. There was a sound like… loose flesh, slapping against bark.

From the darkness beyond the lantern light, something screeched. A shrill ululation that sent knives of pain through her skull, such was the wrongness of it. Creel and the other mortals staggered, clutching at their heads. Some dropped their weapons and collapsed; others maintained their discipline, but only barely.

'Shieldwall! Form the shieldwall!' Aetius bellowed from the line. 'Pull the mortals back!'

Sigmarite crashed as the rest of her cohort advanced to the line of stakes, thrusting those mortals too slow to move behind them. Serena caught a Freeguilder by his cuirass and yanked him out of the way. She caught sight of Creel doing the same, dragging his dazed warriors out of the path of the Stormcasts.

'Go, sister,' said Gardus. 'Take your place in the shieldwall.'

He was already turning away as he spoke, and a moment later he was shouting orders. Serena turned and hurried back to the line. She slid into place smoothly, swinging her shield out and locking it rim to rim with those of the warriors to either side of her.

Ravius chuckled. 'You are moving up in the world, sister. Speaking with the Steel Soul himself.'

'Aye, and why not?' Serena said. 'He is our lord, and we are his warriors. The least we can do is speak to one another.' And perhaps, she thought, even listen on occasion.

Ravius laughed, but a ringing thwack from Aetius' hammer against his shoulder-plate silenced him.

'Did I say you could laugh, Ravius?' Aetius growled as he stalked past. 'Something about this amuses you, does it? Eyes front, mind clear, hand steady. Laughter comes with victory, brother, not before.'

He stopped behind Serena, but said nothing. She kept her eyes resolutely forward, not giving him any excuse to chastise her. Out in the dark, something was watching them. She could feel its gaze on her, sliding across her armour like an oil slick.

'There's a light out there,' Ravius murmured.

'Flux-fires,' Aetius said softly. 'The attack was intended to make us stand still long enough for them to muster enough bodies to bury us. They'll come quick, now that they have an idea of our numbers, and in strength.'

Serena could hear them now, creeping through the dark. A low, pale mist slithered between the trees and surged about the Hallowed Knights' legs like the ghost of a river. It brought the stink with it, and she swallowed, trying to clear her mouth of the taste. The mist wasn't natural. There were shapes in it – ghostly, leering faces with flapping mouths.

The phantoms washed over the Stormcast battle-line, gibbering silently, but otherwise harmless. She heard shouts from behind her, and the crack of a handgun going off, followed by the bull-bellow of an angry sergeant berating whoever had let their nerves get the better of them.

'Hold,' Aetius said. 'We are the bastion upon which the storm of Chaos breaks.'

In the darkness between the trees, something shrieked. A wild, ululating call: a cry of challenge, and of summons. The sound cut through her like a knife.

Behind her, Aetius – steady Aetius – raised his hammer. 'Who will face the ruin of all things, and not break?'

'Only the faithful,' Serena said. She was echoed by Ravius and the others, the words running up and down the line.

Only the faithful. The words were more than a battle cry. They were a mantra. A prayer, a plea and a promise. The warriors of the silver-clad ranks of the Hallowed Knights were chosen for their faith in the face of damnation and death. They were the martyrs of Sigmar, warriors who had fallen in battle with his name on their lips or with great faith in their hearts. That faith bound them after their Reforging more tightly than any earthly chain. They were the faithful, and they would hold back the enemy. They could do no less, if the Mortal Realms were to survive.

More flux-fire flashed in the dark. She could hear screeching, inhuman voices, raised in song – no, a chant. The air became thick and rancid. A sour pong gave vibrant edge to the omnipresent stink, and there came a sound like black thunder, pounding at her ears.

Then the night was split by a daemonic cacophony. All other sound was drowned out by the bellicose roar, and the ground shook beneath her feet. It felt as if something – many some-things – were stampeding towards her.

The first of them appeared a moment later. The creatures had tubular bodies, balanced on a flabby skirt of fungoid flesh. Their flesh sprouted gnashing maws and wailing faces, seemingly at random. Flames spurted from the tooth-lined stumps at the ends of their flailing limbs. They hopped forwards through the trees with ungainly speed, accompanied by loud whooshes of discoloured air. The world seemed to shrink away from them as they lolloped towards the shieldwall, and Serena felt an instinctive chill.

Daemons. She had fought daemons before – the putrid servants of Nurgle, who came stumbling on stick-thin legs, their swollen bellies dripping pus, accompanied by clouds of flies. But these were something different. Something worse, for familiarity bred contempt, and she had never faced anything like these creatures before.

A daemon bounded towards her on its rubbery trunk, hiss-ing and spitting eldritch fire. The flames washed over her shield, and the sanctified metal grew unpleasantly warm. She swung the shield aside and lunged, her warblade punching into the twisting, unnatural form. The daemon squealed and flames cascaded across her armour, scorching the silver black. She tore her blade free in a welter of ichor, and kicked the thing backwards.

'Hold the line, brothers and sisters!' Aetius roared. 'Not one step back, whatever comes. Who will hold the firmament suspended, though the world crumbles?'

'Only the faithful!' Serena shouted, joining her voice to those of her brothers and sisters. 'Only the faithful!'

More daemons tumbled between the trees, spewing their multi-coloured fire across the wall of shields. She raised hers again as a wash of heat enveloped her. The sorcerous fire clawed at her sigmarite, seeking its weaknesses. It slashed out, enveloping the nearby trees and scoring the ground. She heard her brothers and sisters roaring their defiance as the shieldwall began to buckle against the relentless pressure. She set her feet and shoved back against the strength of the flames.

'Only the faithful!'

For a moment, the flames slackened. Daemons fell, as warblades and hammers rang down with terminal finality. The Stormcasts hacked and battered at their foes, driving them back. From behind her, she heard cries of alarm.

'The trees – they've set fire to the trees,' Ravius roared, slashing at a persistent daemon. It clung to his shield, rings of teeth gnawing at the metal.

Serena risked a look around and saw that he was right. In every direction, the forest seemed to be ablaze. Multi-hued flames shimmered along the branches and trunks of the pine trees, causing them to groan as if in distress.

She felt a pressure on her foot, and looked down. A black root had surfaced from the ichor-soaked ground. It resembled nothing less than the head of a questing leech. Shouts and curses filled the glen, as more roots tore themselves loose from the soil with a wet rasp.

The sound rose up, accompanied by a deluge of creaking and popping. At first, she thought it was the foliage being consumed, but then a tree twisted towards her.

As she watched in growing dismay, its bark split open to reveal a distorted maw of splintery fangs, oozing sap. With a soul-curdling groan, the thing that had been a tree lurched towards her, newly grown jaws snapping hungrily.

CHAPTER FOUR

SPLIT-SOUL

The light of change was beautiful.

Tzanghyr Split-Soul, Great Changer of the Thornhoof Warflock, floated in its embrace. The infinite threads of fate threatened to pull his shade in innumerable directions, but he knew his place and purpose, and he held fast to them – to lose one's self in the Infinite was to risk the ultimate dissolution.

Even so, the light was beautiful.

It was the only truly beautiful thing in the realms. The thrum of colour – every colour – and the subtle thunder of the realm's pulse rose up through him to expand and fill his senses. It was blinding and painful and wonderful, all at once.

He could feel the thunder of ancient drums in his spirit, and see the threads flash like lightning. The tops of the trees glowed as if they were aflame, and bands of impossible colour ran through the soil, growing brighter with every passing moment. The Hexwood was growing. Changing. Its crooked pathways were stretching through black seas of infinity, and soon he and his warflock would follow them into the light.

For now, his shade stalked the shadowy threads of fate which ran through the forest, hunting the scent of prophecy. It was the quickest way of seeing what must be seen, in order to prepare for what was to come. The eyes might lie or misjudge, but the perceptions of the soul were harder to fool. The paths of moment and fortune had been seeded and grown here over the course of centuries, and he walked them without fear. The Hexwood had grown strong as its roots fed on the blood of sacrifices, both willing and otherwise. Soon, it would flower in full. When the rite which was even now underway was complete, its shadow would spread over the cities of men – starting with the one called Hammerhal.

It was Tzanghyr's destiny to spread that shadow. To claw out the beating heart of Hammerhal, and make of it something more fitting: a monument not to failed godlings or their servants, but a citadel fit for the children of change – a bastion of the Great Schemer, from where his designs might unspool and stretch to the far corners of every realm, unthreatened and inviolate.

Nurgle, the Chaos God of plague and despair, had once ruled supreme here. The Realm of Life had been his from roots to canopy, even as he wasted his reign hunting the fugitive Everqueen. His brothers had gazed on the prize with envy, for none among them could claim one of the Mortal Realms as their sole fiefdom. But while Khorne had turned his attentions to the realms of Fire and Death, seeking new challenges, Tzeentch had worked patiently and subtly to undermine his great rival.

Now, with Nurgle's season at last waning and his foetid servants in retreat, it was the time of the Great Schemer. His influence swelled as that of his brother dwindled. Where once stagnation had held sway, now change would rule.

The possibilities swarmed about Tzanghyr like a murder of

crows, whispering into his ears. He saw victory, and tasted defeat. Every action, every decision, was a ripple in the Infinite. New portents were birthed from these disturbances, and he sought them greedily, casting aside those which were of no use. They came faster and faster as the power of change built deep in the black heart of the pine forest.

His shade sped on, weaving between the memories of trees. They belonged to Tzeentch now, but the echo of their former masters was held within them, both as a warning and as a prize. The sylvaneth had been driven out at last, thanks to Tzanghyr's cunning. He had taken their soulpods, and with those, their future. He held it in the palm of his hand, and he could crush it at a moment's notice. That threat had been enough to force the tree-kin to leave the forest, but they still lurked close at hand. Watching, always watching. He could feel the subtle pressure of their attentions on the skeins of fate.

They were patient. And cruel. In a way, he almost admired them. But their time was done: the Hexwood belonged to the tzaangors now, and soon Ghyran itself would belong to Tzeentch. Tzanghyr felt the sharp pulse of magics thrum through him, and he followed the multi-coloured threads to their source near the forest's heart.

Too near. Too soon. It had been foreseen, but even so, he experienced a moment of uncertainty.

He saw the shade of his coven-brother directing the warflocks in *tzaanwar* – the ritual slaughter of those who did not know the light of change. He saw the silver-skins and the soft-skins, held at the place he'd dreamed, trapped in a ring of flame and wood. Some would escape the trap – that too, he'd dreamed. He would be waiting for them.

His coven-brother, Mzek, wove cunning sorceries, calling on old alliances made long ago with the Ninefold Courts of Scintillation. Daemons streamed through the gateways of wood, bleeding from one realm into the next, seeking the prey promised to them by his fellow shaman.

Mzek, Tzanghyr whispered, sending his thought-greeting to his coven-brother.

The other shaman twitched where he crouched atop his daemon-disc, his staff clutched tightly in his claws. His brightly hued plumage stiffened as he grunted in irritation at the intrusion in his thoughts.

Tzanghyr laughed. *How goes it, coven-brother?*

It goes as was preordained, Tzanghyr. It can go no better, and no worse. You would know this, if you were here. Mzek was a sour creature, scarred and bitter. Tzanghyr had outstripped him in influence and power, forcing him into a subordinate position that he chafed in. Soon, if things proceeded as they must, he might seek to redress the balance between them. For now, though, he made an able subordinate.

Beware the bite of the Bright Soul, brother, Tzanghyr warned. *I have seen your end, and I would not be proven right in this instance.*

What will be, will be. I have not dreamed of my death. Mzek clacked his beak in irritation. *Begone, coven-brother – back to your bower. You have your rites to oversee, and I have mine.*

He gestured, and their minds snapped apart, like the ends of a broken thread. Tzanghyr hesitated, and then moved on. Mzek would rise or fall by his own doing. They all would. Such was the will of the Great Schemer.

In his dreams, he had seen the silver-skins come and topple the flux-cairn and the lesser herdstones. That could not be allowed, not when they were so close to victory. The uncertainty grew. The forces of the Bright One were closer than he'd thought – Mzek had let them get too far into the forest before he'd sprung his trap.

Tzanghyr glanced up, past the shimmering canopy, into the sky, and saw not stars but the top of a vast hall, stretching into infinity.

Pillars rose like distant mountains, holding up a curved roof, upon which had been carved a dizzying array of shapes and scenes. These seemed to move and change before Tzanghyr's eyes, and he hurriedly looked away from them. Such sights were not for him. Only those who had the favour of the Feathered Lords could gaze upon the convolutions of the Impossible Fortress without being driven mad.

Great avian shapes, indistinct and immense, were perched among the pillars. They looked down upon him with cold calculation. When they spoke, it was not with words, but in a rush of colour and sensation that soothed his uncertainty. The Feathered Lords were pleased with his gambit thus far. They approved of such audacity, when it served their ends.

Satisfied, he looked away. He was following the right threads. He held the skein of his fate firmly. He was sure of it. He had only to pull it taut, and the true work could begin. Emboldened, he flew on, racing now, following the pulsing glow of the change-light back to the roiling heart of the Hexwood. There, in the great vale, his shade circled the nine crystalline monoliths that erupted from the raw soil like blisters, forming a single crown-like shape. The monoliths towered over him, thrusting outwards in all directions and at all angles, catching the light of the moon and stars above and changing it in unsettling ways.

The ancient flux-cairn was like a blister of festering magic; it was the wellspring from which all his hopes and schemes flowed, the heart through which pumped the black blood of the Hexwood. It was almost blinding in its luminosity, and where its light touched, all things changed. The soil became as water or smoke, and the trees bent themselves into ruinous sigils, or else sprouted curious fleshy protuberances which sang soft hymns to the Great Schemer. Strange shapes moved through the ever-shifting soil – things like roots or worms or both, stretching and streaming outwards and away, deeper into the forest.

At the heart of it all, dozens of tzaangors crouched, pounding on wide drums made from the hollowed-out bodies and stretched skins of daemons, their voices raised in a shrieking hymn of abasement. Others blew wild skirls on pipes made from bones, capering as the mad rhythm of the flux-cairn's song flowed through them. The lunatic tempo rose and fell, like waves crashing against the shore, and with every rising, the light of the flux-cairn blazed more brightly.

Tzanghyr found himself drawing closer to the flux-cairn, though it was dangerous to do so as a bodiless shade – he risked being drawn into it, and his essence devoured by the emptiness between realms. Nonetheless, he slid through the stones, following a softer song than the one that held the attentions of his kin. A subtler melody, and older.

At the centre of the stones, floating within their radiant opacity, was a clutch of shimmering orbs – the soulpods of the sylvaneth. The silvery spheres were the hope of the tree-kin made manifest. Within them lay the potential for new groves of sylvaneth, and where they nestled, life flourished. To Alarielle's servants, they were the most valuable of treasures, to be guarded and preserved whatever the cost.

The soulpods were caught within the flux-cairn, both trapped by it and a part of it. To Tzanghyr's eyes, they were all shapes and none, changing faster than even he – attuned to such transmutations – could follow. They were life itself, and there was no telling what they might have become in time.

Even now, they blazed with the raw stuff of creation. That power was all that protected them from the warping influence of the flux-cairn. Soon, however, it would not be enough. The flux-cairn had been raised around them and drew upon their power, turning it to different ends. The rite currently underway would drain that power entirely, and the soulpods would be consumed at last and their essence drawn into the cairn. Whatever was within them would be consumed as well, the whole of its potential devoured and used to fuel the twisted machinations of Tzeentch.

Tzanghyr could hear the soulpods crying out for their protectors as the rite grew wilder. And he could hear the sylvaneth as well, somewhere beyond the forest's edge, watching helplessly, gnashing their splintery fangs in impotent fury. They could not risk a rescue attempt – not if they wanted the soulpods intact – but neither could they allow the ritual to proceed. He shivered in pleasure as their helpless despair resonated through him.

He leapt away from the flux-cairn, satisfied that things were as they must be. He swept beyond the circle of drummers and pipers, seeking the place where his body lay under guard. He looked down at himself, lying curled in a foetal ball upon a bed of moss and branches, steaming braziers arrayed around him. Their contents began to bubble and froth as he dropped down towards his form.

The tattoos which covered his blue flesh began to squirm in welcome, and his crimson mane of plumage flared and flexed as he slid inside himself. Breath flooded his lungs, and he lurched upright, gasping. For a moment, he saw his surroundings through two sets of eyes, and heard the music through two sets of ears. Then his soul settled within his flesh and he was whole again. His limbs trembled with weakness.

'Kezehk – water,' he rasped.

A shape crouched beside him and handed him a clay bowl filled with brackish water. He slurped it eagerly, wetting his beak, and nodded his thanks to the tzaangor. Kezehk was the most loyal of his supporters, though loyalty, like all things, was prone to change at the whim of the gods.

'What did you see, Split-Soul?' Kezehk croaked. The thread-like filaments that encircled his dull eyes twitched slightly. The aged aviarch was all but blind, but his other senses – both physical and magical – had expanded to compensate. 'Victory for the war-flock?' Even crouched, he loomed over Tzanghyr, his form swollen with magical strength. His flock of Enlightened waited nearby, and Tzanghyr could smell their eagerness.

The hulking tzaangors were paragons among the beastkin. They wielded spears wrought of change-metal and saw the echoes of the past-yet-to-be with a clarity that Tzanghyr was envious of. They were warriors without equal, each capable of slaying many lesser foes. They each bore a shard from the herdstone somewhere on them, on their war-plate or embedded in their scarred flesh. To them fell the honour of guarding the flux-cairns, and they had performed this task well under Kezehk's command.

'Always victory, even in defeat,' Tzanghyr said, stretching his aching body. 'All have purpose in the Great Plan, though we see it not.' Such was the way of things, and he took comfort from it. Even failure had its place, though victory was always preferable.

'Yes, yes, but what did *you* see?' Kezehk asked, testily. 'The Great Plan will be as it will be. What does today bring for *us*?' He thumped his chest with a big fist.

'Fire. Flame and spark. The flux-beacon has been lit, and the Grand Vizier calls out to us, from across the twisting path.'

Kezehk gave a caw of laughter. 'Grand Vizier, eh? He grows vainglorious, that one.'

Tzanghyr snorted and rose to his feet. Kezehk stood with him.

'It is the way of them. They know not the beauty of the light, and so cloak themselves in shadow. Names within names. But useful, for all their foolishness. They serve the machinations of the Feathered Lords no less than we.'

'Aye, they serve. And I grow eager to do the same.' Kezehk thumped the soft loam with the butt of his spear. 'Battle calls to me, Split-Soul. I would walk the war-road.'

'And you will, sooner than you might think.' Tzanghyr turned away. 'The silver-skins will come. They will seek to topple the flux-cairn. We must be ready to meet their fortune with ours, and break their destiny beneath the weight of our own.'

Kezehk cawed in satisfaction and thumped the ground again. 'That we can do. Our destiny is heavier than stone, and sharp besides.' His warriors screeched in agreement.

'As sharp as fate,' Tzanghyr said. He caught hold of Kezehk's beak and brought their skulls together with a gentle crack. Their horns scraped and the shaman stepped back. 'But fate cuts both ways, flock-brother. Be wary.'

Kezehk nodded. 'Always, Split-Soul.' He laughed. 'But you worry overmuch. My path is set, whatever comes. What will be, will be, and I follow it gladly.'

He turned to snarl orders to his warriors. They would guard the approaches to the glade, and hold back any who sought to approach unbidden. Tzanghyr knew they would do this even if it meant their death, such was their devotion to the light of change and the Great Schemer's design.

Leaning on his staff, the shaman approached the flux-cairn where it cast its strange light across the clearing. He ignored the drummers and the dancers. Being so close to it inflamed his senses. His strength swelled, but his ability to concentrate dwindled. No matter. Tzeentch gave, and Tzeentch took away. All things served the Great Plan. He reached out to brush his claws across the shroud of iridescent lichen covering the closest of the stones that formed the flux-cairn.

When he looked into the crystal, he did not see his own face reflected back at him. Instead, he saw that of a soft-skin: his coven-brother, the mortal known to some as Rollo Tarn, and to others as the Grand Vizier. The reflection was part of the bargain he had made, so long ago, before the sylvaneth had been driven out and he and his kin had claimed the Hexwood. It was a shard of his coven-brother's soul, resting within his own.

Soul-bonded and bound, their fates were a single thread, stretching into the future. Where one went, the other would follow. Such had been the terms of their bargain, and it had served them well in the years since.

Tzanghyr placed his palm flat against the flux-cairn's surface.

'Coven-brother,' he said. 'Can you hear me?'

Rollo Tarn turned as the apparition appeared in the stateroom of his airship, the *Hopeful Traveller*. He had a goblet of wine in one thick hand, and took a sip before speaking.

'Hello, coven-brother,' he said warmly, nodding to Tzanghyr's shimmering form. 'You look well.' He held out the goblet. 'Care for some wine?'

Tzanghyr cocked his avian skull. 'I am not here.'

'I know – I am being polite.' Tarn took a sip. He frowned. 'It is terrible, at any rate.'

'Then why drink it?'

'Someone has to.' Tarn took another sip. 'Is something amiss?'

'Things proceed as they must, here. The crooked path aligns with the skein of fate, and we will soon follow it. Will we find welcome, when we reach its end?'

'You will.' Tarn hesitated. 'We are making ready to weigh anchor. Once we are airborne, the ritual will commence. The way will be opened, and the city will be yours.'

'Why have you not begun already?'

It wasn't quite an accusation, and Tarn took no offence. Tzanghyr was impatient – understandably so. Nonetheless, he paused before answering. Sometimes, his coven-brother needed his beak tweaked.

'We had visitors. I was hoping to deal with them before we began.'

He restrained a grimace. In truth, he had intended to stage the ritual in the warehouse, surrounded by the blessed wood he had retained for that very purpose. But the invaders had made that impossible. Instead, his acolytes would have to settle for the ship's hold. No matter. He could feel the strength of the rite growing, despite the interruption. Soon, every door would be flung wide, and the servants of the Changer of Ways would sweep through the city.

Tzanghyr cocked his head, one dark eye fixed on Tarn. 'Visitors?'

'A witch hunter. And a Stormcast Eternal.'

'A silver-skin?' Tzanghyr demanded.

'Yes. Gaudy brute.' Tarn swirled his goblet. 'My followers are dealing with them now. Vetch has them trapped in the warehouse. I have faith that he will see that they pose no further interruption to our schedule.'

What the curseling lacked in wit, he more than made up for in tenacity. There were few threats Vetch couldn't deal with, in his own inimitable fashion. He had claimed the souls of more than a few of Tarn's enemies over the years.

'Why did you not alert me of this sooner?' Tzanghyr hissed, plumage rattling. 'They could endanger everything we have worked towards.'

'It is being handled.' Tarn frowned. He had miscalculated somewhat, true, but he saw no reason to admit that, not even to his coven-brother. 'Vetch is perfectly capable–'

'The curseling is a brute and fool. It is why he is as he is.' Tzanghyr tapped the side of his head. 'His weaknesses condemned him to a lesser fate...'

Tarn stiffened. 'Careful, coven-brother,' he said.

The old hurt flared anew, buried so deep he sometimes forgot it was there. Vetch hadn't always been Vetch. Tarn remembered a baby's smile and a child's laugh, and a father's pride at his son's accomplishments. No, Vetch had once been someone else, someone better. But the thread of his fate had been cut, and woven into a new pattern – one more pleasing to the Changer of Ways. But that was slim comfort, even to a man like Rollo Tarn.

Tzanghyr hesitated. He clacked his beak. 'Forgive me, coven-brother. I spoke out of turn. Allowed my impatience to colour my words.' He placed a hand over his heart. 'But you must hurry, or all our efforts will be undone. The trees are the doorway. We open the path from our end, but unless you open it from yours as well, our forces will be lost to the tangled pathways between worlds.'

'The ritual will proceed, coven-brother,' Tarn replied. 'Vetch will not fail. I will not fail you. As you have never failed me. Our thread is one.'

Tzanghyr nodded. 'Our thread is one. My kin and yours.' He looked away, as if at something occurring over his shoulder. 'I must go, coven-brother. I have my own battles to fight. May the Feathered Lords give you strength.'

'Go with the blessings of the Great Schemer, Tzanghyr.'

A moment later, the image of the tzaangor shaman wavered and popped like a soap bubble. As it faded, Tarn touched his chest. He could feel a strange yet comforting warmth there, where his heart ought to be. It came from the shard of Tzanghyr's soul which rested within him, lending him some of his coven-brother's strength, and vice-versa. But would it be enough? Time would tell.

'I can smell the bitterness of your memories from here, coven-brother.'

Tarn looked up, smiling slightly. 'Not bitterness, Aek. Regret.'

Taller than Tarn, Aek had to stoop to fit beneath the state-room's ceiling, and even seated, he loomed. He was so still and silent that Tarn had half-forgotten that he was there. Aek could be quite unobtrusive, when he put his mind to it, which was a handy skill to have for a servant of the Great Schemer.

Aek had served Tzeentch longer than either Tarn or Tzanghyr.

He had served many covens, and participated in many schemes. When he had first arrived in the city, in secret, Tarn had been wary. But in the years since, Aek had proven himself as loyal a coven-brother – and as loyal a friend – as Tzanghyr.

The fatemaster was clad in heavy baroque armour, and wore silken robes worth more than the airship they currently lounged aboard. His conical crested helm rested by his feet, leaving his pale features and long, colourless hair exposed. He smiled easily at Tarn, his black eyes shining with good humour.

'Regret is the spice of a life well lived,' he said.

'I prefer plain foods. Predictable.'

'There is no sin in that. What man does not want a predictable life? Though you may have chosen the wrong god to serve, if that is the case.'

Tarn snorted. 'Who said I chose him?'

Indeed, it was more the other way around. It was Tzanghyr who had saved him from the wrath of the monstrous sylvaneth. The tree-kin had almost taken everything from him, for the crime of simply trying to make his fortune. If not for Tzanghyr and the Changer of Ways, his path would have been short indeed.

Tarn frowned, remembering those early days. He looked around his stateroom, with its sumptuous carpets and expensive carvings, and then at the rings on his fingers and the stitching on his robes. Once, the thought of such luxury had been inconceivable.

A hard life, then. He'd come from Azyrheim with little more than the clothes on his back and the strength to swing an axe. He had been a forester in the Nordrath Mountains, as his father and his father's father had been, but the promise of new realms, of new forests to tame, had been too much to resist. So he'd left. There were opportunities in Ghyran, if you were brave and canny enough to take advantage of them. He'd seen a need and filled it. Soon he was paying others to swing axes, rather than doing it himself.

He flexed his hand. The old scars and calluses earned through a life of hard labour were still there – reminders of the path that had brought him here, to his ultimate opportunity. Even though he'd had men to do it for him, he'd still swung his axe day in and day out, right alongside them. A point of pride, at the time, and one that had almost led to his death.

Tarn took a deep gulp of wine, and felt it burn its way down his gullet. The day he'd set his sights on the Hexwood had been both the worst and best day of his life. A day of great change and opportunity – the very things he'd come to Ghyran to find. But the cost…

His hand tightened on his goblet, and the soft metal buckled. The tree-kin had slaughtered his loggers and stalked him for days, playing on his hope of escape in order to draw out his torment. Their rasping laughter had driven him near to madness. Sigmar had not answered his prayers for aid, his pleas to see his wife, his children, just once more.

But something had. And he served that something now, out of gratitude as much as greed. The Great Schemer was a patron to the ambitious, and the rewards were great indeed, if one could walk the path without slipping. He set aside the crumpled goblet and cast his mind outwards, feeling for the strands of Vetch's dim consciousness.

There was pain, there, and the jagged ever-present pressure of the tretchlet, T'vetch'tek. Not all curselings were subservient to their daemonic symbiote, but most were. Vetch was not one of the rare few with the strength of will to maintain a separate consciousness. He was a hollow thing – a receptacle for magic and the will of the Changer of Ways. He could smell lies and seek out hidden magics – it had been Vetch who had learned how to link the two ends of the crooked path, and to make the lumber taken from the Hexwood into a gateway. In the end, that secret had cost him everything.

'It cost us both,' Tarn murmured. He peered through Vetch's eyes, watching as he fought in the coven's name. 'But is it worth it?' He returned his gaze to Aek. 'Sometimes I wonder.'

'Life is an endless dance of change, coven-brother. We must follow the rhythm, or be lost. You followed. And for that, you and Tzanghyr will be rewarded.' Aek tapped the hilt of the immense two-handed blade standing upright before him. 'As I was.'

Tarn glanced at the blade, and felt a twinge of unease. Known as the Windblade, the great weapon was a cruel-looking thing, all barbed convolutions and squirming lines. The hilt resembled the stretched wings of a bird, and the pommel, an avian skull. Strange colours, such as he had only seen in dreams, ran through the metal of the blade. As Aek's fingers stroked it, the hilt seemed to flap its wings. Tarn suspected that the Windblade had a mind of its own, and that mind was a cunning one.

Aek chuckled. 'It does and it is,' he murmured.

Tarn wasn't surprised that the fatemaster knew what he was thinking. Aek's talents were many. He often finished other's sentences, as if he knew what they were going to say before they said it.

'It has had nine hundred masters,' the fatemaster continued. 'It has been broken and reforged nine thousand times, across ninety-nine thousand years. Sometimes, I feel those other wielders, as if they and I are but facets of a whole. We all grip this blade as one – nine hundred hands, and nine hundred wills.'

'No wonder you can lift the blasted thing so easily,' Tarn said lightly.

Aek chuckled, and for a moment, Tarn thought he heard a chorus of laughter and saw other faces, some not human at all, superimposed over Aek's own. But the moment passed, and it was only Aek there once more. His coven-brother. His friend.

An alarm bell began to ring above deck. Tarn set his goblet

aside. He felt a sudden wrenching sensation, accompanied by a sharp pain in his skull. Images of silver and fire swept across his mind's eye, and he staggered. Aek rose and steadied him.

'Coven-brother?'

Tarn pressed his fingers to his head, trying to massage some order into the chaotic flood of sensations surging through him. He could feel Vetch's dim-witted panic as the battle turned against him. He sent the impulse to turn and fight arrowing into the curseling's stunted mind. If Vetch could hold them, just long enough for the airship to cast off, then he would have served his purpose.

'Forgive me, my son,' Tarn murmured.

Great opportunity only came with great cost. Thus said the Feathered Lords.

'What is it, Rollo?' Aek asked again. 'What has happened?'

'It seems we are discovered. We must cast off now. We cannot risk being caught here. The crooked path must be thrown open. The city must fall.' Tarn pushed away from the fatemaster. 'Ready yourself, Aek. For war has well and truly begun.'

CHAPTER FIVE

FIRE AND AIR

The gryph-hound snuffled at the floor. The blood trail had stopped suddenly, deep within the maze of log stacks and support beams, as if the curseling had vanished entirely.

Carus glowered about him. 'Gone,' he said, his voice echoing.

'So it seems,' Gage replied. 'It led us a merry chase. We should have caught up to it.'

Somewhere behind them, he could hear Kuva and Bryn giving good account of themselves against their foes. He longed to go back and help them, but he knew that tracking the curseling was more imperative than killing a few acolytes. Capturing the creature might enable them to find its master, if Carus could compel it to talk. At the very least, they might learn why every stack of wood in the warehouse seemed to be suddenly sweating daemonic ichor.

He glanced at a nearby stack, lip curling in disgust. The smell, like tar and sugar, clung to every scrap of wood in the place.

'Witch-stink,' he murmured.

The air had gone muggy and thick. It felt like breathing soup.

He had experienced such unnatural heat before, though thankfully only rarely. It built in places of foul magic, like a pot being brought to boil.

'We are being watched,' Carus said.

Gage gripped his sword tightly. 'More acolytes?'

'No. These are not human eyes.'

The Stormcast turned, head tilted as if scenting the wind. Perhaps he was. Carus' senses were greater than those of a normal man, as were his strength and fortitude.

Gage looked around. 'Daemon, then.'

Every instinct he possessed was telling him to get out of the warehouse – to find the others and run. Burn it, as Kuva had suggested, and purge the entire docklands if necessary. Some among his order would not have hesitated to do just that, but Gage preferred subtler methods of investigation. Though he supposed subtlety was no longer an option, in this instance.

'Perhaps,' replied Carus. 'Perhaps something worse.'

'There's nothing worse than daemons, in my experience.'

Carus chuckled. There was little humour in the sound. 'Let us hope that is the case.'

Gage shot him a glare. 'You didn't have to come, you know.'

Carus looked at him.

'Of course I did. The protection of this city, the sanctity of its soul… They are my responsibility. The Hallowed Knights swore an oath – Hammerhal Ghyra will not fall while the faithful stand.'

In the dark, something laughed. The sound rose and fell in arrhythmical fashion, as if it were made by two voices, laughing out of synch.

'Hammerhal*Hammerhal* has*has* already*already* fallen*fallen*.' Like the laugh, the words were out of synch and echoed strangely. Two voices – one impossibly deep, the other almost a screech.

Zephyr snarled and turned, scenting the air. Gage heard a

walkway creak somewhere above. The logs in a nearby stack shifted. Something dripped across the floorboards with a steady sound that invaded his head and made it hard to concentrate.

'Kuva was right,' he said softly as he drew his pistol. 'We should have burned this place.'

The deep voice rose again, this time in a guttural chant. Motes of greasy light danced across the stacked logs. The rough bark split and twisted into grinning faces. Zephyr screeched, and Gage turned to find the animal staring at a nearby support pillar. The flat surface of the wood had a glimmering crack running vertically down its length. As they watched, several wriggling pink shapes emerged and bent like hooks to grip either side. Then, with a rough, wet sound, the aperture widened perceptibly. The light within flared, and Gage gagged as an eldritch stink wafted from it. A bulbous, unformed head thrust out, and eyes like lanterns fixed on him with hateful intent.

Gage recognised the creature easily enough – every knight of the Order of Azyr was made to learn the many thousands of distinct, lesser daemonic manifestations. Some were more common than others, like the daemons known as horrors, and easier to draw up from whatever coruscating hell they inhabited. The pink horror flexed its too-wide hands and crouched on stubby legs as it emerged fully from the rift, which shrank back to a vaguely shimmering crack behind it. The daemon chuckled as it eyed Gage, its worm-like tongue lolling over its ramparts of teeth.

It made as if to speak, but Carus swung his staff up and lunged. The Lord-Veritant drove the staff into the daemon's gaping mouth, shattering many of its teeth. He forced it back, pinning its fleshy form to the pillar it had emerged from.

'Who will carry his light into the dark?' he said, twisting the staff. The daemon gagged, clawing at it, groping uselessly for the Stormcast's hands. 'Who will gaze into damnation's heart unblinking? Only the faithful.'

There was a sound like an overripe fruit bursting, and the daemon seemed to deflate, its pink form dissolving into flame. Its body split and slid from the staff, only to form into two new, smaller creatures – blue horrors.

The blue-skinned little daemons grumbled belligerently as they scampered away, trailing flames in their wake. Gage shot one before it could escape into the dark, and it splattered like hot oil. The bits of flaming flesh writhed for a moment, before a group of even smaller shapes took form, coalescing out of the fire. They scattered like burning insects, and the sound of their high-pitched giggles echoed eerily about him.

'Daemon filth,' Carus said.

Zephyr snarled. The gryph-hound crouched, her feathers ruffled, tail lashing. Her eyes were wide with rage. Ugly chortles rang out around them. Gage holstered his pistol and drew his second one.

'I think they heard you.'

He heard a thump from above, and looked up at the closest stack of timber. Pink limbs were squeezing out from between the uppermost logs, followed by the rotund torso-heads of the horrors themselves. More pink horrors were oozing from the other stacks on all sides of them. Eldritch flames dripped down the logs and crept across the floor.

Many of the horrors seemed to lack the strength to manifest fully, but others had no such difficulties. Chortling daemons reached for Gage and Carus, trying to trip them up or casting flashing spirals of energy at them from their fingertips. Gage swept his sword out, trying to force them back. Steaming ichor spilled from the wounds his blade made, the blessings woven into its steel biting deep into daemon flesh. Zephyr snarled and snapped at the protesting blue horrors when the smaller daemons got too close.

'Carus,' Gage said, 'I think it's time to use that lantern of yours again!'

The Lord-Veritant drove the ferrule of his staff down, and it cracked against the floor. Holding it there, he began to intone a prayer. His words beat upon the air like hammer blows. The Lantern of Abjuration began to glow with a holy light as Carus summoned its full power. The daemons worked more frantically to pull themselves free of their wooden hiding places. They jeered and chuckled, but their eyes rolled with what Gage hoped was inhuman panic. They knew that the light of the lantern would banish them, if Carus could complete his prayer.

One of the horrors, quicker than the others, leapt for the Lord-Veritant, hoping to interrupt him. Gage slid between them, second pistol levelled. He fired, blowing a chunk from the horror's rubbery skull. The daemon staggered, burbling in rage. Then, more swiftly than he could follow, it leapt again, blurring into a frantic streak of glowing colour.

Gage lunged to meet it. Ichor washed over him as his blessed blade pierced its form and disrupted its cohesion. It split into azure shreds, and two blue horrors tumbled away, complaining vociferously. Zephyr leapt upon one, savaging the squealing daemon into burning tatters. The other began to weave its hands in a ritual fashion, but before it could complete its spell, a heavy form trod on it, splattering it like an overripe blueberry.

The curseling thundered out of the dark between stacks, flail swinging. Carus staggered as the creature struck him a glancing blow, interrupting his prayer. The Lord-Veritant spun his staff, trying to drive the creature back, but it pressed its assault. The flail cracked down, smashing the helm from Carus' head, exposing his dark features and a mane of wiry hair bound back in a thick plait. He dropped to the ground and rolled aside as the flail slammed down again, snapping floorboards.

'Carus!' Gage tried to go to his companion's aid, but he was surrounded. The daemons seeped up out of the stacks, clutching at him and giggling like demented children. He slashed at them, hoping the blessed steel of his rapier could harm them. Outsize fists cracked against his back and shins, causing him to stumble.

Zephyr leapt onto the curseling, her beak tearing at its exposed flesh. The tretchlet chattered and struck at the gryph-hound with its staff, swatting the animal away.

'Now*Now* you*you* die*die*, servant*servant* of*of* the*the* single*single* path*path*,' the curseling roared, the tretchlet echoing every word.

Its flaming sword chopped down. Carus caught the blow on his staff. The force of it drove him to one knee. The crackling flames coiled about the staff and the Lord-Veritant's forearms, scorching his silver war-plate black.

The tretchlet waved a hand, and a bolt of sorcerous light burst from its palm. It struck Carus and dissipated into streamers of colour. Thin strands of lightning raced along the length of his staff and crawled along his armour. The daemonic homunculus screamed in agitation and began to thrash on its roots, its fury shaking the curseling. The brute groaned and lifted its flail, ready to bring it down on the pinned Stormcast.

Gage fought desperately to free himself from the daemons. Lashing out with his fists and feet, as well as his sword, he momentarily broke loose. Stumbling slightly, he snatched his knife from his belt and sent it spinning towards the curseling. The blade sank into the curseling's unarmoured wrist with a meaty thunk. Like his sword, Gage's knife had been blessed by the hands of the Grand Theogonist herself, and a thick steam erupted from the wound. The curseling's hand gave a spasm, and its flail fell to the floor. The brute turned, roaring in pain, and tore its blade loose from Carus' staff forcefully enough to send him tumbling to the ground with a crash of sigmarite.

It lurched towards Gage, trailing blood from its wounded hand. The tretchlet screamed imprecations and pounded a thin fist against the brute's helmet, as if trying to stop it from pursuing Gage. The witch hunter retreated, and the curseling pounded after him, smashing aside daemons in its haste. Gage backed into a pillar. The flaming sword arced out and Gage ducked aside. The blade bit into the wood and stuck, its fires crawling upwards as the pillar began to burn.

Flames leapt to the logs and grew merrily. Oily smoke billowed. Past the curseling, Gage saw daemons leap on Carus, their laughter tinged with something that might have been hysteria. The Lord-Veritant lashed out with staff and sword, pulping unnatural flesh or separating groping hands from gangly arms. Sorcerous fire washed across his armour, leaving greasy stains on the silver but doing no real damage. More daemons joined the fray, hurling themselves at the towering Stormcast Eternal, trying to drag him down through sheer weight of numbers.

The curseling left the sword where it was stuck in the pillar and groped for Gage. Its bloody hand, the tip of his knife still jutting from its palm, stretched towards his face. Gage fell back, thrusting his rapier at the brute in a vain attempt to hold it back. Its hand missed him, but only just. He scrambled upright.

The broken body of a daemon tumbled past, crashing into a stack of wood and momentarily diverting the curseling's attentions. Gage saw Carus bulling towards them, despite the daemons attempting to restrain him. Their limbs smoked where they clung to him, and he brushed the creatures aside, or crushed them beneath his feet. Daemons scattered before him, yelping in dismay.

'Gage!' Carus cried. 'Leave this creature to me!'

The curseling roared and turned, catching hold of the blade of Carus' sword as the weapon arced towards its head. It forced the Lord-Veritant back a step, even as ichor poured down its wounded palms. Carus cursed and managed to kick the brute in the chest, knocking it against the pillar.

'I have killed stronger foes than you, beast,' Carus growled. The curseling grunted and reached around to wrench its sword free in a gout of burning splinters. Their swords connected, and the curseling's burning blade exploded into a thousand shards. The two warriors reeled away from each other as chunks of fiery metal scattered in every direction.

Gage took the opportunity to slash at the distracted curseling, but his blade merely scraped its armour. The tretchlet screamed and thrust the bladed tip of its staff towards Gage's face, trying to drive him back. The metal glowed white hot. Gage parried the blow and rammed his sword into the tretchlet's torso. It stiffened, a screech dying on its lips. Black ichor burst from its mouth, and the staff fell from its slack grip. It folded backwards, pulling itself off his blade.

The curseling moaned in agony and clutched at its parasitic passenger, as if trying to wake it. At that moment, Carus rose up behind it, his armour all but black with daemonic blood. His sword crunched through its back-plate. He ripped the weapon free in a welter of ichor.

'Avaunt,' Carus said flatly. Daemons edged away as the Stormcast Eternal flicked ichor from his sword blade.

The curseling staggered away from the Lord-Veritant, groaning.

'F-father,' it grunted. 'F-f-father, h-help me! H-help!'

It turned, stumbling, reaching for something Gage could not see. The tretchlet slumped down its back, body flopping limply as the curseling sank to its knees. It fell onto its hands, wheezing. Gage felt sick. He stepped up to the beast, blade gripped in a trembling hand.

It looked up at him. Its gaze was empty of its previous malignity. Instead, there was only brute incomprehension there now, like an animal that could not conceive of its own destruction. 'H-help,' it wheezed.

'Yes,' Gage said. He raised his sword, and thrust it cleanly through the slitted visor of the curseling's helmet, silencing its groans for good. It crashed to the floor and lay still. He jerked his blade free.

'Well struck,' Carus said.

Gage had no time to reply. Even with the curseling dead, the daemons were still coming. They seeped from the logs and rose up from the floor, their forms twisting and expanding as they burst through the multi-coloured smoke that was beginning to fill the warehouse. They laughed and clambered over the curseling's body, as if its death meant nothing more to them than a momentary amusement.

Carus lifted his staff, and his voice echoed like thunder as he completed the prayer of banishment that had been interrupted earlier. He slammed the ferrule down with an echoing crack. The azure glow within the Lantern of Abjuration brightened, then speared out to blinding brilliance. Shadows were burned away, and the half-formed daemons with them. In the sudden silence, Gage could hear the clash of weapons and Bryn's deep bull-bellow. He hesitated.

Carus caught his shoulder. 'We cannot tarry, Gage. These are delaying tactics. They are trying to hinder us.'

Gage shook off the Stormcast's grip. He was right. It had been a trap, and they had walked into it. They'd stumbled on more than just a cult. This was something bigger. A sick feeling grew in his gut.

'The airship.' He looked at Carus. 'The airship, Carus – we have to get to the airship.'

He turned, and started in the direction of the quay-side doors of the warehouse. The fire started by the curseling's blade was beginning to spread, leaping from log stack to stack. Smoke choked the air, blotting out even the daemon stink.

'Why? What is it?' Carus asked as he loped smoothly in Gage's wake.

'You're right – this trap wasn't meant to kill us. It was meant to delay us, to buy time for the airship to slip its mooring and cast off. I only pray there's still time to stop them!' He hoped Bryn and Kuva would have enough sense to get out before the warehouse burned down around them. 'There – the doors!'

He pointed. The huge double doors were meant for moving heavy logs through. At the moment, they were closed and barred with an immense square beam. Carus put on a burst of speed.

The Lord-Veritant's blade slashed down through the beam, splitting it moments before his shoulder struck the doors. They slammed open with a deep boom of abused wood. Smoke flooded out into the open air. Gage ran after Carus, and saw the *Hopeful Traveller* in all its glory.

The airship resembled one of the low-slung galleys that plied the waters of the Verdant Bay, save that its masts bore no sails. Instead, they connected to several great green gasbags. These were marked with magical sigils, bought at no small cost from the mages of the Collegiate Arcane. The *Hopeful Traveller* was slowly moving from its berth. Crewmen bustled on the quay, throwing off the anchor chains. They scattered as Zephyr darted towards them, screeching.

'We have to catch it!' Gage shouted. Carus nodded.

They raced along the quay as the airship slid from its berth. The ship was picking up speed as the anchor weights were cast off, and it edged ahead of them. Gage had a moment of vertigo as he reached the edge of the quay and saw the vast green sweep of the city spin out below him, but he forced it aside long enough to jump. Heart in his stomach, he crashed against the hull. Flailing blindly, he caught hold of the bottom of the deck rail and hauled himself up, muscles straining, heart thudding.

The rail shuddered, cracked and burst as Carus struck it. The Lord-Veritant crashed down onto the deck, staff in hand. Gage fell after him. He scrambled to his feet, kicking his way free of the broken rail. Behind him, he heard Zephyr shriek in frustration as the ship left its berth, leaving the gryph-hound standing on the quay. Gage glanced back as the animal turned away and darted back towards the warehouse. He turned around to see Carus drawing his blade.

'What now, witch hunter?' the Stormcast rumbled.

Carus stood tall, blade in one hand, staff in the other. Gage drew his rapier. The crew ringed them, weapons ready. They clutched a mix of belaying pins, knives and back-alley blades. They were hard-looking, and all bore the ever-shifting sigil of Tzeentch somewhere on their person – as a tattoo, a scar or a badge pinned to their scarf.

'Drop your weapons,' Carus growled. 'Your souls are forfeit, but your lives might yet be ended in a merciful fashion.' The Stormcast thumped the deck with his staff. Lantern light washed outwards, casting strange shadows across the dark wood.

'And when have you ever shown mercy?' The words echoed over the deck. Gage glanced aft. Two figures now stood at the rail, looking down at the lower deck.

One was a heavyset man, richly clad and wearing a golden mask similar to those worn by the acolytes, though more ornate in design, with proportions that seemed to twist and change as he looked down at them. One gloved hand rested on the pommel of the sword sheathed at his side, and he held a gold-topped staff. The staff seemed innocuous at first glance, no different to what any wealthy citizen might carry, but the strange runes that gleamed and crawled along its length were anything but innocent.

The sight of them stung Gage's eyes, and elicited a feeling of deep revulsion in him.

The other figure was tall, abnormally so, and clad in strange, faceted armour that caught the light in odd ways. He wore brightly coloured robes of rich silk beneath the shimmering war-plate, and balanced a long two-handed blade across his narrow shoulders with a studied insouciance. His helm was archaic in fashion, tall and featureless save for a thin slit for vision and a multihued crest of horsehair which rose over it. The light of the lanterns hanging from the masts seemed to bend and shift strangely about the macabre warrior, and Gage found himself unable to look at the being directly. Even so, he could feel the warrior's fell power beating upon the air.

'Well. I don't recall inviting you two, but welcome aboard regardless,' the heavyset man in the golden mask said. Though Gage couldn't see his face, he sounded amused. 'I suppose it's only fitting – what is the point of a grand working without an audience to appreciate it?' He leaned lazily against his staff. 'My name is Rollo Tarn. I'm told you were looking for me.'

'Rollo Tarn,' Gage said, 'surrender yourself, in the name of the God-King and the Celestial Realm–'

Tarn threw back his head and laughed. 'I do not recognise the authority of your tyrant-god, witch hunter.' His armoured companion joined in the merriment with his own hollow chuckles, and Gage felt his stomach lurch at the sound. He was certain now that there was nothing human under that armour.

'Whether you recognise it or not, it has come for you,' Carus growled. He glared about him, and the crew drew back a step. Tarn looked at him.

'Come to burn more innocents on your holy pyres, Stormcast?'

Carus glared at him. 'You are not innocent.'

Tarn spread his hands. 'No. I am not, at that. Not for a very long time, at least. But the blood I have spilled was done so for a great purpose.'

'I've heard that before,' Gage said. 'It's always the way with your sort. But your great purpose inevitably amounts to the same thing – death and ruin. Not today.' He extended his sword. 'Today, your purpose is unravelled.'

Tarn looked at him. 'I think not. Fate is an ocean, and its tides can wear down even the mightiest of mountains. And these tides have been at work for a very long time.'

'The wood,' Gage said, coldly. 'It's cursed.'

'Blessed,' Tarn corrected. 'Every scrap and sliver of it is both gate and key in one. I spent a fortune bringing it into the city, hiding its true origins, ensuring that it was used in every building I could. Now, I will turn the key and throw wide the gate. But first… Aek, bring me the Stormcast's lightning.'

'It would be a pleasure, coven-brother,' the tall warrior said. He stepped up easily onto the rail and then off it, walking across the air as if it were solid ground. He hauled his blade off his shoulder, and it moaned eerily as he swept it about himself.

'That's no normal sword,' Gage said.

'That's no normal warrior,' Carus growled. 'It is a fatemaster – another cursed slave of Tzeentch, and a far greater one than any curseling.'

Gage tensed. Fatemasters were among the deadliest of the diverse servants of the Ruinous Powers. They were fell warriors, infused with unnatural strength and longevity.

The wind picked up, and the ship's rigging thrashed like a wounded animal. Gage could feel it pulling at him, threatening to knock him sprawling. His coat flapped about him, and his boot soles scuffed the deck as he was pushed backwards, step by step.

Carus had no such difficulty. He stalked towards the approaching fatemaster, head bowed against the wind. The Lord-Veritant slammed his staff down, and the wood of the deck buckled and blackened about the point of impact. The air took on an electric charge, and Gage felt his hackles prickle. The Stormcast released the staff, leaving it upright in the deck.

The fatemaster dropped down, quicker than the eye could follow. His blade wailed like a lost soul as it swept towards Carus. The Stormcast interposed his own, and there was a sound like the pealing of a great bell as the swords met.

Crewmembers were knocked sprawling by the reverberations of the blow, and Gage stumbled back against the rail. Lightning snapped and snarled about Carus as he met the fatemaster blade to blade. The daemon-sword keened piercingly, while Carus' judgement blade blazed brighter with every impact. For long moments, the only sound was the crash of metal as the two warriors circled one another, their duel carrying them from one side of the deck to the other.

While all eyes were on the battle, Gage hurriedly reloaded his pistols. His hands moving on instinct, he let his eyes roam. The wood of the deck pulsed strangely in time with every blow. He wondered if the airship was made from the same wood that had been stacked in the warehouse. As if in answer to this thought, two deck boards at his feet bent away from one another like the lids of a monstrous eye, and something yellow and shimmering peered up at him. Its slit pupil contracted as it caught sight of him.

He leapt back as more boards tore away, revealing a fanged maw. A slobbering laugh emerged from the mouth as he backed away. More eyes and mouths and waggling fingers began to emerge from the wood, piercing it as if it were a thin membrane. Indistinct shapes hunched and heaved, straining to free themselves. Coarse laughter filled his ears as daemons swam through the wood in pursuit of him. Only the light of Carus' lantern was keeping them from fully manifesting.

'They're beautiful, aren't they?'

Gage turned, pistol raised. Tarn stood close by, watching him. Too close.

'They're always there, you know,' he said, taking a step forwards. Crewmen surrounded him like an honour guard. 'Watching. Waiting. Tzeentch's hand is at your throat, though you see it not. His servants walk among you, serene and unknown.' He gestured to himself and the crew. 'And now, the time has come for them to reveal themselves. They shall break through again, where they broke through of old, and the cities of men shall burn in prismatic fire.'

'Not if I can help it.'

'You can't,' Tarn said. He laughed, and spread his hands. Scintillating flames blossomed on his palms and quickly engulfed his hands. 'The rite has begun, and the crooked path stretches through Hammerhal Ghyra. The city will belong to the Architect of Fate.'

CHAPTER SIX

HEXWOOD

The daemon-tree lurched forwards on torn roots, flailing its burning branches. Somehow, in some way unknown to sanity, the daemon-flame had twisted the trees into monstrosities. The mouth in its trunk gnawed mindlessly at the air. Goat-like eyes glared from knotholes and a stink of old blood and rotting wood rolled over Serena as she raised her shield. A branch crashed down on the sigmarite, leaving a trail of smouldering sap. She hewed at the branch, trying to ignore the roots that clawed at her legs.

Her warblade drew thick gouts of sap from the tree's branches, and it reeled back, as if in pain. The tree writhed, its trunk splitting and bleeding as it turned away from her to swat Ravius off his feet. He fell onto his back, and only just managed to interpose his shield between himself and a branch. More branches hammered down, driving him deeper into the loam. Roots slithered over him, as if to drag him beneath the ground. Serena moved to aid him. She chopped apart those roots she could while still defending herself, but the more of them she cut away, the more that lashed about her struggling comrade.

Burning trees lumbered into battle all along the shieldwall, shrieking eerily. Heavy branches swept down, leaving behind burning trails of pine needles. Stormcasts staggered or fell, knocked off their feet by heavy blows or tripped up by slithering roots. More of the flame-spewing daemons raced through the gaps made by the trees, seeking easier prey.

Before they got far, a withering volley of crackling arrows struck them down. The arrows streaked across the clearing, punching the creatures back. Serena glanced behind her and saw a cohort of Judicators approaching, skybolt bows humming as the archers nocked and loosed their deadly missiles. Wherever the shimmering arrows struck, lightning sparked and snapped, casting a white glare across the battlefield.

'Eyes forward, Sunstrike,' Aetius said as he shoved past her. He drove the rim of his shield down, severing one of the roots that entangled Ravius. 'And you, Ravius – on your feet. This is no time for lazing about.'

Together, Serena and the Liberator-Prime managed to free Ravius as the Judicators advanced. The Stormcast archers loosed a pinpoint volley into the trees over the heads of the Liberators, snapping branches and opening steaming black wounds in the squirming bark.

Trees toppled, groaning. A second volley swiftly followed the first. The tree looming over Serena and the others split open and burst, scattering burning pulp over them. Even as it fell, a knot of daemons lolloped towards them, spitting flame. Serena only just managed to interpose her shield. She gritted her teeth against the heat as the Judicator-Prime of the cohort moved to aid her.

'Easy, sister – hold it back a moment longer,' he said, his voice mild. He nocked an arrow and took aim just over her head. 'Easy,

easy – there!' He loosed the arrow and she heard a yowl, cut short. The flames diminished and the heat faded; she lowered her shield and quickly thrust her blade into the wounded daemon before it could rise.

She glanced back at the archer. 'My thanks, Solus.'

He nodded genially and drew another arrow from his quiver. 'I'm here to help, as ever.' Solus spoke calmly, as if he were anywhere other than on a battlefield. The Judicator-Prime was a serene presence, and one that many among the Steel Souls looked to for reassurance when things were at their bleakest.

'Took you long enough,' Aetius said, shoving another daemon back. He smashed his hammer into one of its maws and tore its body open. It reeled, hissing. Solus loosed an arrow into it, knocking it backwards in a clap of lightning.

'I wanted to be sure you actually needed help, brother. You can be very indignant about such things, at times.'

Solus nocked another arrow. Around him, his Judicators spread out behind the shieldwall. At his command, they loosed a withering volley. Daemons shrieked and spun, setting more trees alight as they came apart in shreds of viscous slime and shimmering motes.

As the last of the daemons dissipated, the warped trees tottered towards the shieldwall. Somewhere beyond them, Serena could hear the sound of running feet and the crash of metal on metal. Screeches and howls echoed up; the tzaangors had regrouped, and were using the lurching trees as cover as they raced towards their foes.

She was forced to step back as a heavy branch slammed down, nearly crushing her flat. Nearby, a Judicator screamed as a jagged branch punched through a gap in her armour. She fell, her form reduced to crackling sparks of azure lightning. A Liberator was dragged bodily out of line and into the mass of trees, where he vanished from sight. His curses dissolved into howls of agony before another blue bolt soared skywards. Roots lashed through the gap he'd left, slamming against the warriors to either side, causing them to stumble. The shieldwall was beginning to fray beneath the unyielding assault.

Serena jerked her shield up over her head. A branch splintered itself against it. 'We have to fall back!' she shouted.

Aetius nodded, but before he could reply, the ground began to shake. Serena turned and saw Gardus' bodyguard of Retributors advancing quickly to the fore, Feros in the lead.

'Step aside, brothers and sisters!' he roared. His voice echoed through her like the rumble of thunder. 'It is time to gather some firewood.'

The Paladin Retributors advanced as a solid wedge as the Liberator shieldwall dispersed. When they struck home, the wedge flared and opened, revealing Lord-Celestant Gardus in their midst. His light blazed forth, and the corrupted trees cowered back. Their newly sprouted eyes rolled and their twisted mouths gibbered as the radiance washed over them.

The Retributors, led by Gardus, went to work. Wherever their hammers struck, a tree toppled, or burst into cleansing flame. Gardus' own tempestos hammer snapped out. Lightning flashed through the glade, and a twisted tree splintered. It toppled with an almost human groan, branches flailing.

'On the final day, who will remain?' the Lord-Celestant roared. 'Only the faithful!' Feros and the other Retributors echoed him, their voices rising up over the sound of destruction.

As the last of the ambulatory trees fell, a tzaangor leapt over it and swung a two-handed blade at the Lord-Celestant. Gardus parried the tzaangor's blade and smashed the creature from its feet with bone-breaking force.

'Who will guide the lost from the dark of despair?' he cried. A second tzaangor was sent sprawling, neck snapped, as it slunk out of the mist and smoke. 'Only the faithful!' Gardus lashed out with a boot and kicked a tzaangor backwards. As it stumbled, he caved in its skull. 'When the strength of men fades, who will yet stand?'

'Only the faithful!' Serena responded, her voice joining that of every Stormcast within earshot.

She clashed shields with a charging tzaangor and knocked the beastkin sprawling. She stamped on its chest, crushing its sternum, then turned to meet the charge of another. The avian monsters flooded out of the trees, attacking with a singular ferocity. Solus' Judicators chose their targets with precision, trying to stem the assault, but slowly the line of Liberators and Retributors was being driven back by the sheer press of bodies. Only Gardus held his ground, and neither daemon nor beast could touch him.

For a moment, his light blazed forth, brighter than the moon above, only to be snuffed out by a vivid firestorm that engulfed him and his bodyguards with a colossal roar of sour light and strangling heat. Feros, on the fringes of the blast, was knocked to one knee, parts of his war-plate fused to slag. Several of his cohort were sent hurtling back to Azyr before they even had a chance to scream. Gardus himself was hurled back into the battle-line, his armour smoking. He crashed through the shieldwall, knocking several Stormcasts sprawling.

Half a dozen flying shapes screamed out of the smoke and flame. The tzaangors were mounted on daemonic disc-like creatures. Some of the discs resembled spinning sawblades, while others looked like tailless lampreys studded with barnacles of bone. Several of the tzaangors carried bows, while others grasped barbed spears. The one in the lead bore no obvious weaponry, but seemed all the more dangerous for it. Unlike the rest of its foul kin, the creature was clad in shimmering robes and bedecked with thick plumage. The air bubbled and twisted around it, as if the world itself were trying to reject the creature.

'Shaman,' Aetius spat.

The tzaangor shaman hurtled across the clearing over the heads of the stunned Stormcasts. Crouched atop its whirring disk of brass and silver, it gestured with its crooked staff. Blue flame cascaded from its tip, enveloping a nearby knot of Freeguilders as they rushed to bolster the battle-line.

The soldiers screamed as their flesh darkened, and they collapsed to the ground, tearing at their uniforms. Feathers burst from their flesh, and their skulls cracked and split, lengthening into new shapes. Serena watched in horror as the mortal warriors were twisted into braying tzaangors. The creatures lurched to their feet, still clad in the rags of their uniforms, and lunged at their former fellows. Several of them peeled off and rushed for the wagon on which the *Impertinent Maiden* sat.

The helblaster volley gun gave a roar, and the rushing tzaangors were reduced to bloody pulp and mist. The crew hastily began to reload as a tzaangor disc-rider shrieked out of the thickening mist. The beastkin whipped past them and separated their heads from their necks with its spear in a spray of red. Smelling blood, the ghyroch pulling the wagon snorted and began to gallop away, spilling shot and supplies from the back as it went.

Lightning crackled as Solus' Judicators loosed a well-timed volley. The disc fell, writhing sickeningly, arrows jutting from its underside. The tzaangor rider hit the ground and rolled, squalling. Freeguilders closed in on it as it clambered to its feet, but were driven back by its barbed spear. It fought with a savage skill, moving more swiftly than the mortals could match.

Serena glanced at Aetius, who nodded tersely. 'Go,' he said, taking her place in line.

She raced towards the creature, moving as fast as her war-plate allowed. It turned at the last moment, thrusting its spear towards her. She caught the blow on her shield, and guided the barbed blades over her shoulder in a spray of sparks. She drew a line of blood from its side, and then they were moving in a tight circle. Spitting unintelligible gibberish, it spun its spear, the weapon seeming to leave phantom afterimages in its wake. The tzaangor thrust the spear at her again and again, driving her back.

As she blocked its blows on her shield, she saw more of the disc-riders hurtle through the walls of flame. These carried cruel-looking bows rather than spears, and they loosed as skilfully as any Judicator did. A Liberator was punched from his feet, an arrow jutting from the eye-slit of his helm. As he fell, his form dissolved into lightning and surged upwards. More daemonic arrows thudded into a bellowing ghyroch, slaying the dumb beast in its tracks. Arrows punched into the ground around Serena, sending her stumbling back.

Her opponent leapt forwards, cackling as its disc-riding brethren swooped by, seeking new prey. The spear twisted, gouging deep lines across the face of her shield and nearly tearing it from her arm. She turned with the blow, and slashed at the beastkin. They moved back and forth, trading blows. It was faster than she was, and that speed only seemed to grow as the fight went on. Their blades connected, and she felt the reverberation not just in her arm, but in her soul as well. It shook things loose within her, brief fragments of the past dappling her consciousness like raindrops. She saw a woman's face – her own, perhaps – and felt a faint echo of melancholy. It slipped away as another blow tore her shield from her.

She staggered back, flourishing her warblade to keep her opponent at bay. It lunged again, but lurched at the last moment as a crossbow bolt sprouted from its neck. Beyond it, she saw Sergeant Creel make the sign of the hammer in triumph, or perhaps thanks. Teeth bared, she took a two-handed grip on her warblade and drove it through the beastkin's chest until the hilt clanked against its armour.

Serena tore the blade free as bow-wielding tzaangors shot past her in pursuit of Creel and his men as they fell back. Retrieving her shield, she moved after them.

The beastkin's deadly arrows tore through several of the fleeing Freeguilders, ripping them from their feet and sending their bodies tumbling like dolls. Creel, despite the awkwardness of his wooden leg, made it into the shelter of a supply wagon. He hauled himself over the side and into the back with ungainly speed.

A line of crossbowmen had formed near the wagon, using it as an improvised rampart. As Creel clambered to his feet in the back of the wagon, someone handed him up a loaded crossbow. The Freeguilders fired at his barked command.

The onrushing discs didn't slow, despite the bolts bristling from both discs and riders. Creel shouted again, and the crossbowmen dropped flat, allowing the halberdiers crouching behind them to rise up and thrust their weapons out. The beastkin were caught by surprise. One of the tzaangors fell from its perch, squalling, and several crossbowmen fell on it with knives and swords. Two died, but the blades of the rest of them found purchase, and the beastkin slumped, its broken bow sliding from its grip.

The remaining disc-rider tried to flee, but Creel raised his borrowed crossbow and let a bolt fly. It caught the tzaangor between the shoulder blades and knocked it from the sky. His men cheered as the thing rolled to a stop near Serena. She lopped its head off as it tried to rise, and raised her bloody blade in a terse salute. Creel responded in kind.

A wash of heat across her armour caused her to turn. She saw the tzaangor shaman swooping over a group of Stormcasts. Its fiery magics splashed across their armour, staggering them, but otherwise doing no harm. Judicator arrows slammed into its disc, and the circular daemon-thing convulsed and shrieked. The shaman leapt lightly from its daemonic mount as it fell, wracked by lightning.

The shaman landed and swept its staff out, unleashing a lash of flame that drove nearby Stormcasts and Freeguilders back. It cawed harshly, and began to weave a spell. Serena hurried to intercept it, but Gardus reached their foe first. The Lord-Celestant stepped through the shaman's flames without hesitation.

His armour still smoked from earlier, and his sigmarite warcloak was in tatters. Streaks of soot and ash marred the golden ornamentation. But his light still burned, and as he scraped the blade of his sword against his hammer, the flames thinned.

'This forest is not yours, beast,' he said, his voice carrying easily through the glade.

'Not yours either,' the creature crowed. It pointed its staff at him and traced abominable sigils on the smoky air. 'You will not claim Mzek's plumage, Bright Soul, whatever others might have dreamed. I will rip out your lightning and weave it into a chain to wear about my waist, eh?'

'No,' Gardus said softly.

Even so, the word boomed out, as final as an executioner's strike. The shaman cocked its head, as if confused. Then it reared back, screeching in pain. Serena's eyes widened as she caught sight of one of the tattooed tribesmen behind the beast, a bloody knife in hand. While they'd all been distracted, the forester had struck. The shaman spun, shrieking a deplorable word. The forester died in silence, erased from existence by a fiery undulation that left an after-image seared on Serena's retinas.

As his ashes fell to the forest floor, his comrades attacked. The tribesmen leapt on the tzaangor shaman. Knives and hatchets flashed as the savage warriors hacked at the stunned creature. It squalled in pain, and slashed wildly with a hooked knife. As it flung its attackers aside, crude arrows loosed from bows of horn and sinew sprouted from its back and chest. The beastkin staggered, slumping against a wagon. The knife fell from its hand.

The tribesmen stalked towards it, faces hard. Serena made to join them, but Gardus thrust his hammer out, stopping her. 'This kill is theirs,' he said firmly. 'A debt long in the owing, now paid in full. As I swore to them.'

The shaman's screeches spiralled up before breaking off into strangled gurgles. Out in the dark, the thump of drums fell momentarily silent before starting up again, their fury redoubled. Daemonic laughter echoed through the trees, but not so loudly as it once had. With the death of the shaman and his entourage, the rest of the tzaangors had retreated.

'They will regroup soon,' Gardus said. 'We must be quick. Hyrn!'

The tribesman stood. 'Here, lord.' He looked at Gardus. 'There are more beast-witches than that one in this forest. One more, at least.'

'We need to find the seat of their power.'

'It is not far, I think,' Hyrn said, cleaning his knife on his furs. 'There is a place where the forest turns sour, and the wind sings strange songs. It is where they lair. But they will intercept us before we can reach it...'

'Not if we force them to split their attentions,' Gardus said. 'Gather your warriors. You will lead us now, while they are in disarray.' He turned. 'Feros, with me – you will clear us a path. Aetius, Solus – I will need some of your conclaves too. We must find the head of the serpent that encircles us, and crush it.' Gardus looked at Creel, who stood nearby. 'Sergeant Creel. Can you get the *Impertinent Maiden* singing again?'

Creel saluted with a bandaged hand. 'We'll get her caterwauling, my lord.'

Gardus nodded in satisfaction. He looked at the others. 'Hold the line. Hold their gazes here. I don't want them to see the blow that kills them until it's too late.' He met Serena's gaze. 'You – Sunstrike. You will come with me.'

'As you will, my lord,' she said. 'As far as my faith will carry me.'

'To the heart of the forest will be far enough.' He turned to Aetius. 'I need four more. And five from you, Solus.'

'Will that be enough, my lord?' Aetius said doubtfully.

'It will have to be.' Gardus looked at Serena. 'Who will walk through the fires of Chaos unbowed, sister?'

Serena slammed the flat of her sword against her battered shield. 'Only the faithful.'

'Only the faithful,' Gardus said, nodding. He looked towards the forest. 'Let us hope that is true. I fear that this blaze is but the barest edge of an inferno unseen.'

CHAPTER SEVEN

RITE OF THE CROOKED PATH

Rollo Tarn gestured, unleashing his spell, and multi-coloured flames washed over the deck of the airship. Gage threw himself aside and fired one of his pistols. Tarn staggered with a startled cry as a blossom of blood appeared on his robes. He clapped a burning hand to his shoulder and screeched, 'Kill him!'

Tattooed crew members leapt to obey. Gage cast aside the empty pistol and fired the other. Tarn ducked away, and a crewman folded over with a groan. Then the others were on Gage, and he had no time for anything but the fight at hand. Parrying a blow from a cutlass, he drew his knife and retreated, intent on putting the mast at his back.

The crew were tough. Experienced. The veterans of tavern brawls and boarding actions. But he was a knight of the Order of Azyr. With cool, precise skill, he used their numbers against them, as he'd been taught. Witch hunters often found themselves alone and outnumbered, and Gage had learned how to turn that weakness into strength.

As the crewmen closed in on him, he twisted aside, avoiding blows that fell on the men behind him. His rapier lashed out, not for killing blows, but in crippling slashes directed at tendons and hamstrings. Overeager crewmen tripped over their wounded fellows, opening themselves up for his blade. His knife zipped out across wrists and elbows.

However, skill alone wouldn't see him through. He knew that, as surely as he knew that he had to stop whatever rite Tarn had set in motion. Carus' light wouldn't hold the daemons back forever either. The Stormcast might be able to purge the vessel of its daemonic infection, but only if he were given time.

As he fought against the crew, Gage kept an eye on the duel between the Lord-Veritant and the fatemaster. The two warriors seemed evenly matched, but Aek was fresher. The wailing blade he held disrupted the wind with every slash, causing the deck to pitch and yaw. Carus stumbled back, barely interposing his own sword as the fatemaster struck at his head. The echoes of the blow swept across the deck, knocking several of Gage's opponents sprawling. He took advantage of the momentary opening and lunged towards Tarn.

The magister, hand still pressed to his wounded shoulder, thrust his staff towards Gage. The sigils hammered into its length flared with a sickly light. Gage, on instinct, dived aside as the sorcerous blast pierced the space where he'd been standing. It enveloped a crewman who'd been coming up behind him, club raised.

The man screamed as his body tore itself apart. His flesh split like an overcooked sausage, revealing scales and feathers. His bones splintered and reshaped themselves, lengthening and curving. His flesh sloughed away and resurged, colours changing. Eyes and mouths sprouted in the nooks and crannies of his new shape, as thorn-like talons slid from raw, fleshy paws. Bulbous tendrils composed of repurposed muscle and fat lashed out in an orgy of agonised violence. The thing screamed through a thicket of sharp fangs.

Unlucky crewmen were smashed from their feet, or torn apart where they stood. Loyalty to the Dark Gods was no proof against the maddened instincts of the newborn Chaos spawn. It was a thing of pure hunger and instinct, all that it had been consumed in the unholy fires of its creation.

The Chaos spawn lunged for Gage, yowling. He ran, leaping over casks and bundles of rope, and darted behind a mast. The Chaos spawn blundered after him, splintering the deck boards with its heavy body. It caught hold of the mast and swung itself around, its stretched maw opening in a roar.

Gage dropped flat as its claw lashed out. The mast shuddered as the beast struck it. Gage turned, caught hold of a mast line and chopped through the knot holding it secure. He was jerked off his feet and yanked upwards as the rope slithered through the pulleys above. The Chaos spawn shrieked and pursued him, scrambling swiftly up the mast.

Gage slammed into the mast, on a perch just beneath the bottom of the gasbag. He let go of the rope and caught hold of a guide line, preventing himself from plummeting back down to the deck below. He tried to think of some way of defeating the creature rapidly ascending in pursuit. There were any number of blessed sigils and sacred talismans in the pockets of his coat, but he doubted they would do any good.

Mind racing, he glanced up across the night sky, back towards the aether-dock. A thin shape was visible – a skycutter. The smaller vessel was a graceful blade, its aether-sails pushing at the air like the wings of a falcon. The skycutter arrowed towards the *Hopeful Traveller*, and Gage's heart leapt as he caught the faint sound of a duardin sky-shanty, ringing out from the approaching vessel.

'Bryn?' he muttered.

The skycutter caught the wind and surged forwards, closing the gap. No one had noticed it yet, being too distracted by the Chaos spawn's rampage. Gage glanced down as the creature hauled itself closer. Its bulk was still realigning itself to its new shape, slowing its ascent. It lashed out at him with a spiny tendril, and he slammed back against the mast to avoid it. Its claws tore into the perch, and he stabbed at them with his rapier. A tendril tipped by a snapping maw shot towards him, and, using the guide line for balance, he ducked aside, swinging out over the deck. He pinned the tendril to the mast, eliciting a shriek from the Chaos spawn. The monster began shaking the mast, trying to free itself.

Gage ripped his sword free, and the beast screamed as it made to haul itself up onto his perch. Before it could do so, the skycutter crashed into the side of the *Hopeful Traveller* with a tooth-rattling roar. Timbers bent and burst, and the airship thrashed like a wounded animal. Crewmen were flung screaming from the ship, and Gage was nearly hurled from the mast. The Chaos spawn wasn't as lucky. It tumbled to the shattered deck below with a bellow.

Through the smoke of the impact, Gage could see that the skycutter had lived up to its name – its reinforced prow had chopped into the side of the *Hopeful Traveller* like a knife blade. The smaller vessel hung in place, embedded in the larger airship. It had torn a gouge in the deck, deep towards its centre. Stunned crewmen started towards the vessel, even as others ran to try and steady the *Hopeful Traveller*. The airship was listing badly, its hull creaking. Shouts of alarm filled the air. Gage wondered how much longer it would hold together.

'Ha-ha!' Bryn bellowed as he dropped down from the prow of the skycutter, a pistol in either hand. The duardin's armour was scorched and stained, but he seemed to be in one piece. '*Khazukan Khazuk-ha!* The duardin are on the warpath, and your debts have come due!'

The drakefire pistols roared, and crewmen fell. Bryn holstered the weapons and unslung his hammer, swinging it out in a bone-crushing arc. He trod over the bodies of the fallen, accompanied by the gryph-hound Zephyr.

'Ho, Gage! You can come down now – I am here, and you are safe.'

'I'm not worried about me, Bryn – watch out!' Gage shouted down as the Chaos spawn rose unsteadily to its feet. Its many eyes fixed on the duardin, who turned to face it.

'Come on then, you ugly–' he began.

A double-bladed axe spun through the air, embedding itself in the spawn's skull. The creature stiffened, whined and slumped. It seemed to deflate as Gage watched. Kuva leapt lightly from the skycutter and reclaimed her axe.

Bryn glared at her. 'He was mine.'

'There are plenty of other things to kill.' Kuva nodded to Gage as he climbed down from the mast. 'You caught the curseling?'

'We caught more than that. The skycutter?'

'We borrowed it from the dock when Zephyr came to find us.' She bestowed a rare smile on him. 'I had forgotten how much fun they are to fly.'

The smile vanished as quickly as it had surfaced. She spun, axe chopping through a crossbow bolt as it streaked towards her. The crewman who'd been holding it backed away, hastily attempting to reload. Kuva pursued him, frowning.

Gage looked at Bryn. 'Help Carus.'

Zephyr was already loping across the deck, following the ringing clash of blades. Carus and his opponent ignored everything else, intent only on each other. They moved through the smoke, easily holding their balance on the swaying deck as their swords connected again and again.

Bryn frowned and peered at the duel. The fatemaster raced

through the air, and Carus met him, blade to blade. Gage and Bryn had to turn away as lightning flashed.

'Doesn't look like he needs any help to me,' the duardin growled.

'It's a distraction. I need him to help me undo whatever rite they've begun. Help him.'

'And what'll you be doing, while I'm doing that?'

'What I can.' Gage started towards the rail and the wound that the skycutter's arrival had opened in the *Hopeful Traveller's* starboard side. He had not seen Tarn since the crash, but it was too much to hope that the magister had been one of those killed in the impact.

Sheathing his sword, he climbed out over the rail. The wind tore at him, and he caught a glimpse of the city, spinning out below. From this height, it looked like the rings of a tree. Moving carefully, he kicked aside broken hull planks and clambered through the hole, down into the ruptured hold. He was acting on instinct now; Tarn had mentioned a rite, but there had been no evidence of one in the warehouse, or above decks.

A curious sight greeted him as he dropped beneath the broken deck. A circle of nine acolytes, dressed much the same as those they had fought in the warehouse, sat in a wide circle around an alchemical flame, burning up from a large, flat crystalline plate. Braziers had been arranged about the hold, but several had been knocked over, scattering burning coals. The wood smouldered.

Despite the condition of the hold, the edge of the skycutter's prow thrust into their sanctum, and the rush of the wind, the nine acolytes paid no heed to anything save the flames. Their hands moved in ritual gestures, and their voices, hoarse with effort and exhaustion, were raised in a chant. They looked wasted, somehow, as if they had not eaten in weeks. Their golden masks sat strangely on their faces, and their robes hung loosely.

Gage had seen similar sights before. They were feeding

something of themselves into whatever rite they were conducting; it was draining them of life, so it could grow stronger. But as to what the rite was, he could not say.

In the false light of the flame, he could see different parts of Hammerhal, the images floating like soap bubbles above the crystal plate. In one, the door of a tavern split like a new scab as something tubular and frenzied wriggled out into a packed common room. Daemonic flames washed across the startled patrons, consuming them. In another bubble, the back wall of a stable began to shudder as pink shapes burst from it like maggots from a wound. The chuckling daemons fell on the screaming horses with a monstrous enthusiasm.

Sickened, Gage looked away. It was the same in the other bubbles – and not just daemons, but twisted beastkin as well. Tzaangors erupted into filthy alleyways and temple naves, and they immediately set about slaughtering anyone who crossed their path.

More bubbles rose from the flames: tens, dozens, hundreds. In each, similar scenes played out. In the barracks of a Freeguild regiment, in a duardin delving tunnel, inside the warehouses of the aether-dock – anywhere and everywhere Tarn's wood had been put to use, daemons and beastkin emerged from the flat planes.

'Gate and key, as I said.'

Gage looked up. Tarn walked down the steps on the other side of the hold, followed by several crewmen.

'The God-King's witches harnessed the volatile emanations that nestle in the bedrock of this place to create protective wards about the city. Wards which are proof against even the most cunning magics, as others have discovered to their detriment, time and again. However, I long ago learned that there is no problem money cannot solve.' Tarn rubbed his fingers together for emphasis.

'You brought the wood in, sold it to unsuspecting buyers and somehow opened a path through the city's defences,' Gage said, circling the chanting acolytes, keeping them between himself and Tarn. There had to be some way to break the spell.

'It took years. But I learned patience in service to the Changer of Ways.' Tarn lifted a sheathed sword into view. 'I learned many things. Like the best way to harvest cursed wood from a god-touched forest and use it as a pathway back to that same forest. Though granted, I had some help with that.'

Gage lifted his own sword. The crewmen descended and spread out around him. Daemonic faces leered at him from the walls and beams of the hold, laughing silently at his predicament.

'You think you've won, don't you?' he said.

Tarn laughed. 'No. This is but the beginning.' He drew his sword and gazed down its length. Ugly, gash-like sigils marked the blade. 'This city is well defended. But there is an army on the other side of the gate – the blessed children of change wait for us to open the way from this side. Hammerhal Ghyra will fall to the warflocks of the Hexwood. Then, Hammerhal Aqsha. And after that – who is to say?'

Gage shook his head in disbelief at such hubris. Men like Tarn always spoke with conviction, even when they said the same words a hundred men before them had already said, and a hundred men after would say too. It was always the same. Domination. Conquest. Hubris.

His sword still extended, Gage cast a quick look around. He needed a distraction.

The deck above bowed and burst, raining jagged chunks of planking down on the congregants. They did not cease their chanting, though slivers of wood pierced the chests and arms of several. Tarn stepped back, cursing, as Carus and the fatemaster slammed into the floor in a cloud of splinters.

'That'll do,' Gage said.

The two warriors were on their feet almost instantly, neither giving ground. Their swords crashed together with hurricane force, and daemon-winds lashed through the hold. Crewmen were lifted and hurled back against the hull. The flames snapped and surged.

'Aek, take the fight away from here – we're too close now!' Tarn howled. He drew his own blade and lunged for Carus.

Gage intercepted him. As their swords scraped together, Gage caught hold of Tarn's robes and swung him into the flames. It wasn't pretty, but it was effective. Tarn screamed in agony as the mystic fire blazed up, seemingly consuming him. Hearing his screams, the fatemaster glanced around, as if in concern. Carus seized the opportunity, and his judgment blade crashed down on his opponent's helm, splitting the metal.

The fatemaster groaned and swept his sword out. A typhoon of wind sprang up and caught at Carus. Slowly, the Lord-Veritant was forced back by the building tempest. His armoured boots dug shallow trenches in the deck as he was pressed back towards the place where the skycutter had impacted the *Hopeful Traveller*. The smaller vessel shook as the mystic winds lashed it. With a trembling roar, it was ejected from the hull of the larger airship, hurtling away and down towards the city below.

The winds built to a screaming crescendo. Carus spun his blade and stabbed it into the deck in an attempt to anchor himself. Even so, Gage could see that it wouldn't hold for long. Unless he acted quickly, the Lord-Veritant was going to be swept out of the hold.

He lunged, thrusting his rapier through a gap in the fatemaster's armour. The creature stiffened and whirled, dragging the winds along with his blade. Gage was flung backwards, perilously close to the flames; he rolled aside, only just managing to avoid them. As he rose to his feet, he saw that the eldritch flames had spread, consuming the circle of chanting acolytes. Their seated shapes burned like hunched pyres. They hadn't even tried to escape. The spell had consumed them utterly – there would be no easy way to break it now.

He turned back to the fray as a hurled axe struck the fatemaster in the chest, knocking him flat. Kuva leapt down into the hold, reaching for the haft of her axe. The fatemaster lurched up, driving her back. He tore the axe from his chest and cast it away. The aelf ducked aside as the warrior hacked at her, and his blade split a support beam. The hold groaned as the flames crept higher. More of the heat blister images formed. They drifted through the hold, momentarily distracting the combatants. Among the new images, Gage saw a forest and the silver-armoured forms of Hallowed Knights, locked in battle with tzaangors and daemons. Whatever was going on, it wasn't isolated to Hammerhal Ghyra.

Blades slammed together with a crack of steel. Carus had regained his feet, and the fatemaster met him. Even wounded, the servant of Chaos seemed determined to prevent them from interfering with the flames in any way.

Kuva caught Gage's eye from across the hold. She glanced up, and he saw Bryn standing above, at the edge of the hole in the upper deck. The duardin lifted a pistol meaningfully. Gage nodded, and he and Kuva moved to flank the fatemaster. Carus wouldn't thank them, but that was a problem for later. Needs must, when daemons drove.

A drakefire pistol roared from above as Bryn made his contribution to the fray. The fatemaster staggered. He turned, eyes glazed with pain.

'Nowhere to go,' Gage said, lifting his rapier. Kuva raised her axe and stepped forwards. Carus stepped back, a disgruntled look on his face.

The fatemaster tore off his battered helmet, exposing pale, saturnine features, covered in blood. 'There is always another path,' he said, smiling slightly. Then, with a single awkward step, he dived into the flames, dragging his screeching blade in his wake.

Startled, Gage made no move to stop him. The flames blazed up, licking at the walls, and the fatemaster vanished. Whether dead or simply gone, Gage couldn't say, and he didn't particularly care at that moment.

'Carus – we may need your lantern,' he shouted, gesturing to the flames. 'Whatever they've started, I know of no way to stop it.'

'We have to destroy this ship,' Kuva said, glaring at the flames.

'That alone will not be enough,' said the Lord-Veritant. 'The daemons have already breached the wards of the city. We must collapse the paths they've created and draw them back into the Realm of Chaos.' Carus stared into the flickering flame, his face set, his expression grim. He whistled sharply and Zephyr appeared in the hole above, head cocked. The Lord-Veritant looked up. 'Bring me my staff,' he called out. He steadied himself with his sword as the hold shook.

Gage frowned as he caught hold of a support beam. The ship felt as if it were about to shake itself to pieces. 'Can you do it?'

'If I could not, I would have suggested something else.'

Gage looked up as the bubble containing the image of a warrior chamber of Hallowed Knights fighting in a forest drifted by. Was that the Hexwood that Tarn had mentioned? The only Hexwood that Gage knew of was a forest on the slopes of the Nevergreen Mountains.

A harsh sound filled the air – a scream of pure, infernal malice. It ripsawed through them, and Gage staggered, hands clamped to his ears. Even Carus shuddered, squinting against the monstrous pressure. Only Kuva didn't flinch. She looked around.

'Daemons,' she said flatly.

'Where?' Bryn demanded from above.

Even as he spoke, something long and pink erupted from the

splintered end of a broken plank and swiped at him. The duardin jerked back with a curse as the pink horror hauled itself towards him, a twisted grin on its malformed features. His hammer snapped out and crushed its head. It flopped to the deck, still partially merged with the wood.

Daemonic chortles echoed through the planks, and ugly faces swam across the interior of the hold. Hands and talons oozed out of the grain of the wood on all sides, reaching for them. Gage stabbed a leering face as it bulged towards him, bursting one yellow eye.

'Carus – whatever you are planning, make it swift,' he said.

A muffled shriek sounded as Zephyr reappeared, clutching Carus' staff in her beak. The gryph-hound leapt into the hold, bounding from broken plank to beam, agilely avoiding the burning talons of the daemons that swiped at her. Carus caught up his staff and slammed the ferrule down. Light blazed from the lantern, bathing the hold. For a moment, the daemons retreated. But only for a moment.

'Go,' he rumbled. 'Get above decks.'

Gage hesitated. 'What about you?'

'I am where I must be.' Carus met his gaze. 'Much is demanded of those to whom much is given. The time has come to pay down that debt.'

The fires roared up suddenly, licking across the ceiling and spreading across the floor. Gage and Kuva were driven back towards the steps leading to the upper deck. Carus gestured with his sword. 'Zephyr – go!'

The gryph-hound shrilled, as if in protest, but leapt over the growing flames to join the others. As they backed up the stairs, Gage's sword split a daemon's leer, and Kuva's axe finished it. Blue horrors rose from the bubbling remains, and Gage punted one of them into the spreading fire. The other was split into two burning, cackling daemon-flames by Kuva. Gage stamped on them, snuffing them out.

Over the spreading flames, he saw Carus raise his staff. The Lantern of Abjuration glowed with a light that rivalled that of the flames. The Lord-Veritant was chanting as daemons rose up around him, bleeding from the floors and walls. The creatures tore at him, their cackles taking on a frenetic quality. Lightning bled from his wounds and crackled within his eyes. His voice thundered above the wind and the howling of daemons. His sword slashed out, spilling daemon-ichor, as his prayers reached their crescendo.

'Come, Gage, hurry,' Kuva said, catching Gage's arm and hauling him up the steps. 'Whatever he's planning, we won't survive it this close.'

He allowed the aelf to pull him out of the hold, but he couldn't look away from the Lord-Veritant's final stand. The flames encircled Carus like the talons of some great beast. His cloak burned away to ash as Gage watched, and his armour blackened and warped, its gilding dripping away as the sigils etched into the plates glowed white hot. But still he stood, holding his ground against innumerable foes and the heat of foul magics. Azure light bled from him, rising in crackling motes from his armour and exposed face.

Despite all of it, he was smiling. That was the last sight Gage had of him, as he scrambled above decks with the others. Bryn hurried towards them.

'The crew – what's left of them – scrambled the driftboats a few moments ago,' he said. 'Think they know something we don't?'

Cobalt lightning lashed upwards through the holes in the deck. It ravaged the masts and upper decks, tearing at the wood. Somewhere, daemons were screaming – not in joy, now, but in pain. And, Gage hoped, fear. Whatever Carus was doing, they didn't like it.

A moment later, a column of lightning blazed upwards through the deck, scattering boards in all directions and nearly deafening Gage. One of the masts cracked and slammed down, knocking them all sprawling. Overhead, the gasbag rippled as lightning tore across it, leaving burning punctures in its wake.

Daemons tried to free themselves from the wood, only to be caught by the strands of lightning and hauled back towards the hold, dragged screaming into the radiance that burned there. This was not the sickly glow of the ritual fire, but a purer light: the light of Azyr, of Sigmar's cleansing storm, unleashed at the heart of whatever ritual the foe had enacted. The ship bucked beneath the touch of the lightning. Whole sections of the hull cracked and fell away, raining like burning comets over the city.

Gage looked at Bryn. 'I don't suppose there's a driftboat left?'

Bryn grinned and patted his hammer. 'I thought you might ask that, so I made sure of it.'

He turned and clambered off, moving as fast as his thick legs could carry him. Zephyr bounded ahead of him, screeching in encouragement, and Gage and Kuva followed as quickly as they could. The *Hopeful Traveller* was cracking apart even as it drifted over the city. Lightning crawled across the shaking deck, as if urging them on.

The driftboat was a curved leaf of massive proportions, folded and shaped by the Greenpriests of Hammerhal Ghyra into a vessel which could catch the wind and carry its occupants safely to the ground. It hung from the side of the rail, and they hastily clambered aboard, settling themselves on the rounded benches. Kuva's axe easily sliced through the ropes holding it attached to the airship, and Gage's stomach leapt into his throat as they dropped away from the lightning-wracked hull of the *Hopeful Traveller*.

The city rose swiftly to meet them, before the driftboat caught the wind and levelled out. Below them, Hammerhal Ghyra was burning – or at least parts of it were. Even from such a height, Gage could hear the crack of gunfire and the bellicose grumble of Ironweld artillery.

'He's dead, then,' Bryn said, watching as the *Hopeful Traveller* succumbed to the forces within its hold. The night sky blazed bright for a moment as the airship exploded and the last of the lightning savaged its way towards the stars and Azyr. 'That sort of lightning only crackles when one of Sigmar's chosen falls.'

'Yes, but in death, he's beaten them,' Gage said, and knew it was true. The raw power of Carus' sacrifice would surge through the mystic pathways that Tarn's cult had created, hopefully collapsing them. Without constant reinforcements, the remaining daemons and tzaangors would swiftly be overwhelmed by the city's defenders.

'Not all of them, I hope,' Bryn said. 'Be a dull affair if we go through all that and miss the battle because we're too busy riding a flying leaf.'

Kuva laughed. 'There are always more daemons to kill.'

'She's right.' Gage leaned back. 'Somehow, I think we'll find a way to keep busy.'

He reached out and stroked Zephyr's flat skull. The gryph-hound settled beside him, chirping. If she was dismayed by the fate of her master, she gave little sign. Then, perhaps she knew she'd see him again, sooner or later. Gage looked up, watching as the burning wreckage descended across the horizon.

'Hurry back, my friend,' he murmured. 'I fear we'll need your light again, and sooner than we think.'

CHAPTER EIGHT

FIRES OF LIFE AND HEAVEN

With Hyrn and his Verdian tribesmen leading the way, the Steel Souls' march through the Hexwood was swift. Around them, the pine trees shook, as if caught in a great wind. Wisps of light danced across their tops and flames licked at the horizon, as the battle in the glade began anew. Serena wondered whether Creel, Shael and the others in the Faithful Blades regiment would survive the coming hours. For a Stormcast, death was inevitable – they had been forged to die, and die well. But mortals were more fragile. The Stormcast Eternals fought and died so that mortals could live; to see them die so brutally, and so permanently, sickened her to her core.

She tried to push the thought aside. 'Much is demanded of those to whom much is given,' she murmured. The first canticle of the Hallowed Knights, the words by which they lived and fought. Sigmar had given them great strength, and in return, he asked only that they use it in a righteous cause. In *his* cause.

Even as she repeated the words, she caught glimpses of what

might have been faces staring at the marching Stormcasts from knotholes and strange shapes that loped from one trunk to the next, moving within the bark like shadows, keeping pace. Serena tried to ignore them, but they pressed close, and more than once she thought she heard the whisper of voices, just at the edge of her hearing.

The Steel Souls were being followed.

Whether by foes or something else, she did not know, but she suspected the latter. At least twice, their small group had nearly run right into a warflock of tzaangors – loping towards the battle in the glen, or away from it – but the beastkin had not so much as paused, despite the wind being at the Stormcasts' backs. In both cases, Serena thought that the trees had somehow bent, as if to obscure them. As if the forest were seeking to hide their approach from the beasts who now ruled it.

'Halt.'

Gardus' voice carried easily through the dark. Serena and the other Liberators spread out automatically, falling into a skirmishing line among the trees. The Judicators stayed close, arrows nocked. Feros and his surviving Retributors stood at the centre of the line, arrayed to either side of Gardus. They had come to a cleft in the slope where the trees thinned. Great eruptions of rock, marked with strange carvings and sigils, cut through the forest floor, rising like irregular parapets. Thick scrub covered the ground and clung to the rock.

From beyond the stones came the sound of drums, the same ones they had heard at the beginning of the earlier attacks. There was light as well – a watery glow, shimmering up into the murky sky above.

Hyrn spat and unslung his bow. 'This is it. The forbidden vale is beyond these rocks.'

Though he spoke softly, Serena heard him as easily as if she had been standing beside him. The cleft was narrow and unwelcoming: the perfect place for an ambush, or a stalling tactic, depending on how far back it travelled.

'Those carvings on the stones,' Ravius murmured from beside her. He'd been chosen to go as well by Aetius. 'They're sylvaneth. I saw them at the Blackstone Summit.' He looked around warily, scanning the trees.

'And in Gramin,' Serena said. 'But they've been defaced.' The crudity of the desecration offended her, though she did not recognise the original purpose of the sigils.

'Other gods rule here now.' Gardus drew his runeblade. His voice silenced all conversation in the ranks. 'But not for long.' He looked down at Hyrn. 'You and your people will stay here. This battle is not for you. If we fail, you must carry word back to the others.'

Hyrn made as if to protest, but fell silent under Gardus' calm gaze. There was a weight to that gaze, Serena knew – not a harsh or hateful one, but heavy all the same, and few could bear it for long. The tribesfolk melted away into the trees, silent as shadows. Gardus watched them go, and then turned back to the cleft.

'Heavy Hand,' he said.

'Aye, my lord,' said Feros. 'Speak, and we shall do.'

'Make a joyful noise, my brother,' Gardus said, scraping the edge of his blade against the face of his hammer. 'Let them know who has come to call.'

Feros laughed loudly. He slammed the ferrule of his hammer down on a stone and raised the weapon up. 'You heard him, brothers and sisters. Let us sing them the song of our people.'

He started forwards, and the other Retributors advanced with him. As they strode towards the cleft, they slammed their hammers together, weaving a ponderous rhythm. Cobalt sparks flickered with every crash, until the head of each hammer was wrapped in crackling brambles of azure light. The sound echoed up, pushing back against the dolorous beat of the unseen drums like the crash of the sea against the shore.

'Where I walk, no gate shall bar the way,' Feros rumbled. 'No wall, no bastion shall halt my advance. I am faithful, and my faith opens all doors.'

As they reached the cleft, the Retributors lifted their hammers as one. They moved without hurry, but steadily, a millstone of silver and azure. Their lightning hammers snapped out and the rock face… ceased to be. Dust filled the air as the cleft crumbled, and the slope shook. With every impact, more lightning ravaged among the stones, reducing them to rubble or uprooting them entirely.

'Loose formation,' said Gardus as he advanced into the billowing dust, his light acting as a beacon to those following behind.

As they walked, Serena and the other Liberators began to strike the flats of their shields with their hammers and warblades. Behind them, the Judicators' voices rose in song – a hymn from the Age of Myth, remembered now only by a few scattered tribes of desert dwellers and those who had been raised up from among them. The song flew ahead of them, riding the crashing wave of destruction.

The Retributors forged ahead, widening the cleft with every swing of their hammers. The rock face crumbled beneath their assault, and the slope quivered as avalanches were set off nearby due to the rhythmic destruction. Over the noise, Serena could hear the panicked cries of beastkin. Undoubtedly, they had been guarding the path, but there was no defence against such unbridled destruction. As the Stormcasts advanced through the dust, she trod on broken bodies – tzaangors, caught by falling rocks or the ricocheting bands of lightning that erupted with every hammer blow.

'We seem to have ruined their ambush,' Ravius said. 'Pity.'

'There's more where they came from,' Serena said. Somewhere above them, on the shuddering slopes, dark figures raced. Screeching brays sounded as avian bodies leapt down into the dust and thunder, seeking silver prey.

Serena pivoted, and her blade caught a tzaangor in the neck. Its head spun away in a cloud of gore. Behind her, a Judicator fell beneath a swarm of bodies. His essence thundered upwards, and tzaangors rolled away, beating at the flames that clung to them. Ravius crashed into them, scattering them.

Gardus moved through the fray like a pillar of fire. His voice rang out, a clarion call cutting through the noise. 'Whose deeds shall be written upon stone?'

'Only the faithful,' Serena panted, choking on dust. The others echoed her.

She drove a tzaangor back against the crumbling rock face with her shield and slid her blade into its midsection. She let the body fall and stepped back, instinctively seeking the safety of the formation. Maintenance of the battle-line above all else was drilled into the Stormcasts from the moment of their apotheosis. Only by working together as a single mechanism of war could they hope to be victorious.

'Who will find redemption, at the end of all things?' Gardus roared out, somewhere ahead of them. His light flared, and she caught a glimpse of him, surrounded by darting beast-shapes. The tzaangors were drawn to the Steel Soul like moths to a flame.

'Only the faithful!' she cried, advancing to his aid. Arrows shrieked overhead, punching tzaangors off their feet or pinning them to fallen trees.

'Who shall weather the storm of storms?' Gardus called, backhanding a beast with his hammer. He lunged smoothly, spitting another on his blade.

'Only the faithful!' Serena bulled into a tzaangor shield-first as it made ready to strike the Lord-Celestant. She bore it under and stamped on its head, bursting its narrow skull. 'Only the faithful!' she cried again. The words filled her with strength, easing the weariness that threatened to slow her limbs.

'Indeed, sister. Only the faithful.' Gardus wrenched his runeblade free of a dying tzaangor. 'Keep moving, brothers and sisters. Do not slow your pace. Do not hesitate. We are the blade of Azyr, and we seek the enemy's heart.'

The Hallowed Knights advanced as one, following the trail of destruction carved by Feros and his fellow Retributors. The cleft widened into an immense vale, like a wound within the heart of the slope. Trees clustered as thick as a ghyrlion's pelt, rising from the uneven ground in clumps and bunches. Rocks rose among them, thick with phosphorescent moss.

At its heart, a cyclopean circle of crystalline shapes rose from the blighted soil. They loomed like the prongs of some vast, hateful crown, and the light which emanated from them warped everything it touched. A glowing mist rose from the torn earth, faces and shapes forming and dissolving within it. Those trees closest to it had become nightmarish growths of flesh and scale, rather than bark. Their roots twisted and thrashed like snakes, and their branches tore at the air like claws. Serena had seen such a thing before – a flux-cairn, raised by the beastkin over sites of great magic.

Phantasmal daemons capered within the twisted grove that surrounded the stones, singing an abominable hymn. They gave no sign of noticing anything save the monstrous colours pulsing and flickering deep within the milky facets of the flux-cairn. Nor did the ring of tzaangor drummers and pipers show any awareness of the enemy who had come upon them so suddenly. But the vale had more defenders than just bestial musicians and daemons. Tzaangors swarmed through the trees, screeching out war cries as they raced to intercept the invaders to this, their most sacred of places.

As the Hallowed Knights entered the vale, Serena saw that Feros and his Retributors were already locked in battle. They fought with a group of heavily armoured tzaangors, larger than the others and led by an eyeless brute. Feros and the creature strained against one another, their weapons locked.

Gardus stormed towards them, smashing aside any beast that sought to bar his path. 'Who shall carry Azyr's light into the darkness?' he cried.

'Only the faithful!' Serena shouted as she fought at his side.

They were outnumbered. The vale was full of beastkin, but the creatures did not press their advantage as one might expect. Instead, only the bare minimum needed to slow the Stormcasts' advance threw themselves into the fray. The rest of the tzaangors loped into the blazing facets of the monoliths as if they were doorways. The surfaces of the great crystals churned like whirlpools, greedily enveloping the beastkin as they plunged into them.

'Where are they all going?' Serena shouted, bashing a beast from her path. 'Where are they sending them?'

Gardus didn't reply. The Lord-Celestant steadily pushed his way towards the centre of the clearing and the cairn, chopping down or smashing aside anything that got in his way. Feros and the surviving Retributors fought to clear his path against the heavily armoured tzaangors, but there were simply too many of the beastkin. Even with Serena and the others aiding them, their progress was slowed to a crawl.

Then, the eyeless tzaangor broke away from Feros and lunged for Gardus. The Retributor-Prime roared in fury, but found his pursuit blocked by another of the creatures. The tzaangor's spear carved a black trench across the Lord-Celestant's side, staggering him.

'Kezehk has seen you, Bright Soul,' the creature bellowed. 'Seen you in dream and portent. Now Kezehk will slay you, in the name of the Feathered Lords.'

The creature spun its spear with impossible speed, launching blows, driving Gardus back step by step. Off balance, the Lord-Celestant absorbed these blows, turning with them.

Serena and Ravius fought their way to his side. Ravius got there first, and managed to interpose his shield, catching a blow. The force of it knocked him to one knee, and before he could rise, the tzaangor was on him. It kicked him in the chest, knocking him prone, and drove its spear down through his body, pinning him to the ground. Ravius screamed. Lightning billowed upwards, separating the tzaangor from Gardus. It staggered back, losing its grip on its spear.

Furious, Serena drove the rim of her shield into the back of its skull, knocking it onto its hands and knees. There was no finesse to the blow, only anger. As the beastkin shook its head and tried to rise, Serena drove her blade down through its neck.

The creature lurched away from her, gagging. It swept its fist back, catching her on the temple. She fell, her helmet rolling away. The tzaangor stumbled after her, one hand clamped to its ruined throat. It was dying on its feet, but was determined to avenge itself. She pushed herself upright and sprang to meet it. She smashed the tzaangor back and hewed at it. It caught at her shield, gurgling imprecations as she forced it backwards, plunging her sword into it again and again. She lost sight of Gardus – of everything save the creature before her. In that moment, it seemed to be the sum of all that was foul in the Hexwood.

Abruptly, it fell away from her, dragging her shield from her arm. Dead, it toppled backwards into one of the facets of the flux-cairn, and vanished with a sound like a stone falling into mud. Bewildered, she looked around, and realised that she'd somehow managed to force herself a path through the melee. The light of the flux-cairn caught at her gaze, drawing her eyes towards the pearlescent shimmer in its depths.

She could see great pathways of twisted wood stretching backwards into a kaleidoscopic void. The pathways rose and fell with no rhyme or reason, like a tangle of dark thread. Daemons and beastkin raced along most of them, hurrying towards a mote of green light in the distance. Flying monstrosities hurtled through the void above, riders bearing twisted standards hunched upon their backs. She could hear the scream of infernal horns and the crash of war drums. An army on the move, but heading where?

It all made sense now. The tzaangors had never intended to drive them from the wood. This was no army here, but a rearguard, meant to protect this hideous gateway until the last of their forces were on the march. But… there was something else there too. Something at once impossibly far away, and yet within arm's reach.

Entranced, she looked into the heart of the flux-cairn, and saw… *light*. A purer light by far than she'd expected. Silvery shapes pulsed in that light, shapes that were all things and none. There were faces there, childlike and androgynous, calling out for aid. She felt the desperate trill of their song in her bones, and took an unconscious step forwards. The surface of the facet rippled, as if in eagerness.

The sounds of battle faded to a dull clamour. Lightning flashed, casting its glare across the clearing. She took another step towards the light. She felt the song grow in her. Out of the corner of her eye, she saw lean shapes, inhuman but beautiful for all that, watching from among the trees. No – from *within* the trees. They were singing as well, singing to the silvery shapes, calling to them, reassuring them.

Trapped. They were trapped. Prisoners. No… They were *hostages*. She shook her head, trying to clear it, and she raised her warblade. If she could free them…

Pain flared through her, and she staggered. More pain – flames licking over her armour, reducing the holy sigmarite to white-hot slag. She spun, instinct guiding her blade, and sheared through the end of a staff clutched in the talons of a tzaangor. Another shaman, to judge by the primitive decorations it wore. The creature screeched at her as it cast aside the ruined staff and drew its knife. The shaman leapt onto her, knocking her backwards. Her warblade whirled from her grip. The beastkin was stronger than it looked, and its eyes burned with fury.

'You will not!' it shrilled in a croaking parody of a human voice. 'The crooked path will remain open. Open!'

Its knife pierced a join in her armour, seeking the flesh beneath. She grunted in pain and struck the creature. It reeled, beak splintered by her blow. She shoved the creature back and lurched upright. Bleeding, weaponless, she lunged towards it, hands reaching for its throat. The shaman gave a screeching laugh as she bore it back. Why was it laughing?

The song in her head rose to a mournful ululation. There was fear there, and despair. Pain. She glanced at the flux-cairn, and at the shapes within it. They were starting to dissolve.

'Too late,' the shaman hissed, grabbing her. 'They will feed the path with their death. It will remain open.' She didn't understand what its words meant. Whose death?

The blade of its knife threaded a gap, and found her abdomen. She gasped. The edge of her world turned azure, and she wondered if this was what Ravius and the others had felt. Was this what it was like to become one with the lightning, to die again and be reforged? There was blood on her hands, and in her armour. She reeled back, vision dimming.

The song changed. It pierced the fog of pain. She shook her head, listening – truly listening now, for the first time – and took another step back, closer to the shimmering cairn. The tzaangor shaman pursued her, screeching imprecations. She ignored it. Turned. And saw cerulean lightning erupt suddenly from within the flux-cairn. It boiled up from somewhere deep within the green light at the other end of the pathways and cascaded across the crystal edifice, cracking the stones and disrupting the light.

Serena shaded her eyes, and felt the familiar pulse of Azyr within the lightning. Somehow she knew that, on the other end of that daemonic pathway, something disastrous for the foe had occurred. Acting on instinct, she lunged forwards and plunged into the lightning-wracked facet before her.

It felt like diving into a storm-tossed sea. She was buffeted on all sides by unseen forces as she entered the pallid void. In the distance, distracting colours swirled through a great emptiness, broken only by innumerable fibrous pathways, twisting like mangrove roots away from her and into the green distance. The silvery motes hung suspended at the heart of this root-like web, and she stumbled towards them. The pathway undulated beneath her feet, as if in pain from the lightning crawling across it.

More than once, she nearly fell, due to either her injury or the writhing of the pathway, but something kept her on her feet. She felt as if someone were beside her, helping her walk. The wound in her side wept lightning, and it crackled and crawled over the silver surface of her armour, burning it clean of filth. She heard a faint roaring in her ears, and thought it might be a voice, urging her on.

She stretched her hands towards the silvery motes, fighting against the silent winds that swept through the void. She knew what they were now. Soulpods – the future of the sylvaneth race. They cried out for aid, and through her, something answered. Their warmth enveloped her; their song welcomed her. Driven by some instinct she could not name, she gathered them to herself, protecting them against the scouring wave of lightning as it filled the hollow space between moments.

Ignoring the pain, she cradled the silvery pods, hunching forwards to absorb the impact of the lightning. It cascaded across her, and she sank to one knee on the spongy surface of the wooden pathway. Out of the corner of her eye, she saw many of the other twisting pathways crumble, one by one, as the cerulean energies lashed through the ranks of the army attempting to traverse them. Screams tolled in the void like bells, and the sound of splintering wood threatened to deafen her.

Eyes half closed, she huddled, wondering when it would end. The pain in her side grew, spreading through her, and the lightning clawed at the edges of her sight. She heard the plaintive song of the infant spirits in her care, and the voice of the lightning, whispering in her head. She could see a watery reflection of reality back the way she'd come. She rose to her feet and stumbled towards it, intent on carrying her charges to freedom. Around her, the empty place between moments convulsed like a thing alive. Lightning strobed across its impossible dimensions, burning more pathways and streaking off into the iridescent emptiness.

The essence of the void caught at her like quicksand, slowing her. Even as it was consumed by the lightning, it was trying to prevent her from leaving with its prize. She stumbled, and felt the panic of her burden. So close to freedom, and yet… so far.

Then, a beam of light punched through the colourless murk. The voice of the lightning thundered wordlessly in her head and soul, urging her on towards the radiance. A silver gauntlet emerged from within its blinding heart, reaching for her. She caught hold and was hauled out of the void, even as the lightning collapsed the pathway behind her.

Gardus dragged her back into the vale with a shout of triumph. As she tumbled to the bloody ground, her burden slid from her grip. The soulpods rose into the air over the vale, their radiance growing stronger with every passing moment. Where it struck the tortured earth, foulness was cleansed. Twisted trees burst into purifying flame as the steaming soil expelled the sourness within it. Daemons screamed as they were consumed by light and lightning both. They wavered and vanished like burst soap bubbles.

'Up, daughter of Azyr. Now is not the time for rest.' Gardus caught Serena's hand and hauled her to her feet. 'There is work yet to be done, and a war yet to be won.'

'My warblade,' she began. Her body ached, but she felt no weakness. It was as if the lightning had reinvigorated her, drawing her back from the cusp of death.

'Take mine,' Gardus said, drawing his runeblade and passing it to her. He looked at her. 'You did well, sister. Whatever comes of it, know that.'

She nodded her thanks, though she was not sure of just what she might have accomplished. She took a two-handed grip on the runeblade, wondering what had possessed her to do as she had done. It was as if some force, far greater than herself, had guided her actions. She could still feel the heady pulse of it pounding in her veins.

Around them, the battle continued. There were so few of her brothers and sisters now – of the twenty who had accompanied Gardus, fewer than half remained standing. Feros was among them, roaring out oaths as he smashed tzaangors from their feet. The lightning danced across them, lending new strength to flagging limbs. Serena blocked a blow and bisected her attacker from its crown of horns to its gem-studded belt.

Above them all, the silvery shapes grew more distinct as they grew brighter. They contained a multiplicity of possibilities. Some held tall, winding stalks with feathery leaves, while others were heavy with golden, glowing cocoons. Inside still more were shimmering fungal orbs surrounded by haloes of diaphanous seeds. Hundreds of shapes, each stranger and more glorious than the last.

And all of them sang with the same voice: a roaring tidal wave of joy that washed over the vale and set the pine needles to clicking.

Serena heard a screech of denial, and saw the tzaangor shaman fighting its way through the melee towards them, surrounded by a bodyguard of its bestial kin. As the creature wove its claws in a mystic gesture, its followers surged towards Gardus. He turned to meet them, hammer in hand, but before he could strike a single blow, a flurry of movement interrupted them.

In the glare of the light, she saw impossibly quick, thin shapes burst from the trees all around. The sylvaneth were at once humanoid and utterly unlike any living thing. The tree-kin emerged from all sides of the vale, and fell upon the remaining tzaangors en masse.

Bark-sheathed, bladed limbs scythed through tzaangor flesh. Root-like talons propelled lean, trunk-like bodies into battle. Jagged mouths opened in a communal hiss, as branch-laced skulls thrust forwards fiercely. The sounds of the sylvaneth pulsated on the air, like the crash of old trees toppling. Tzaangors died, and those that did not, fled.

'What is this?' Serena asked.

'Something I'd wager that they have been waiting for for some time,' Gardus said.

The shaman was taken by surprise. Sylvaneth fell upon it from all sides, their splintery talons tearing into the startled creature. Their screams were vengeful, rasping things that sent a chill through Serena. The tzaangor gave a despairing shriek and fell, all thoughts of vengeance forgotten. Roots and vines ensnared the creature, dragging it to the ground.

All across the vale, a similar entrapment was taking place. All of the surviving beastkin were afflicted by grasping roots. Some were dragged out of sight, deeper into the woods, while others were jerked, struggling, up into the trees. But most were pulled flat to the ground and then, slowly, beneath it. Their screams echoed through the vale.

Serena watched as the shaman tried to hack itself free of the entwining vegetation with its knife, but to no avail. Slowly, inexorably, the shaman was drawn beneath the churning soil, babbling prayers and curses. Then, it – and all of its kin – was gone, leaving no more than a faint smear of ichor upon the ground.

Wrath sated, the sylvaneth looked up as, with a final roar, the silvery soulpods surged upwards and away into the green skies. There they scattered on the wind like shimmering pollen until they were at last lost to sight. As the light of their passing faded, the first of the stones began to crack and shift. The lightning too had faded, but it had completed its task: the flux-cairn was dying. Its glowing facets had grown dim and cracked. One by one, they began to crumble into glittering fragments.

As the last of them collapsed into dust, the sylvaneth turned to study Gardus and Serena. She hesitated beneath those flat, inhuman gazes. She could still hear their song in her mind, though only faintly now. The tree-kin undulated closer, one reaching out with a barbed talon to push aside her sword. It tapped a claw against her chest-plate, and she looked down to see that strange, knotted patterns – reminiscent of the twisting shapes of the soulpods – had seared themselves into the sigmarite. From the pain in her chest, she suspected that similar markings now scarred her flesh as well.

'What...?' she began. She glanced at Gardus.

'A token of esteem,' he said. He bowed his head to the sylvaneth. 'From one ally to another.' The tree-kin hesitated, and then emulated the gesture. They were not human, but some things were universal.

A moment later, they departed, with only the rustle of loose leaves to mark their passing. They vanished into the shadows between the trees, and were gone.

Serena turned to gaze at the shattered cairn. 'What happened here?'

'I told you,' Gardus said, 'sometimes even the strongest warrior requires aid, even if they cannot ask for it directly.' He pulled off his helmet and tucked it beneath his arm. His hair was white, and though the face it framed was that of a young man, his eyes were old, and tired. But still vibrant. Still faithful.

'But, these cairns… I saw pathways…' She stared at the rubble.

Gardus nodded. 'Perhaps the sylvaneth were not the only ones who needed help. Sigmar moves in mysterious ways.' He looked up at the stars above. 'To defend one realm is to defend all eight. We stand together, or fall separately.' He made a fist with his free hand. 'We are more than Sigmar's wrath, sister.' He opened it again. 'We can also be his hand, extended in friendship. Today, we were both.'

'And what of tomorrow?'

'We are the faithful, and we will stand, whatever the cost.' He looked at her. 'Never doubt that, sister. Whatever the future holds, whatever waits for us there – remember this moment. Remember what you did. That is our purpose, above all others. Much is demanded…'

'Of those to whom much is given,' Serena said. She straightened her shoulders, her fingers tracing the new patterns burned into her armour. Only time would tell what they meant.

Gardus clasped her shoulder. 'What awaits us when the last war is won, and the last march home begins, is a mystery. I doubt even the God-King himself knows. But today, you have brought us one step closer.' He smiled. 'And tomorrow, I have faith we will be one step closer still.'

CHAPTER NINE

THE GREAT GAME

Aek opened his eyes. The howl of eldritch winds had died away, leaving his ears ringing and his skull full of echoes. It had been a risk to leap into the ritual fires. There was no guarantee that they would do anything more than consume him. But Tzeentch loved a gambler, and Aek had seen no other option.

The fatemaster staggered to his feet, the Windblade gripped tightly in his blistered hand. The daemon-blade growled softly, as if in warning. Groaning, he used the blade to lever himself upright. Everything hurt, but the Feathered Lords had blessed him with a durability far beyond that of any mortal. A durability that had been sorely tested this day...

The Stormcast warrior had been stronger than any that he had yet had the misfortune to face. And a passable swordsman, besides. Aek ran a hand through his sweat-matted hair, grimacing at the throb of pain in his skull. If not for his helmet, his head would have been split, and the Windblade in the hands of a new master.

'But not today,' he muttered, tightening his grip on the sword. It quivered in his grip, though whether in pleasure or annoyance, he could not say.

He looked around. He stood in a circle of flame atop a stone dais. Masked acolytes watched him from beyond its glare. They stank of fear. Some bore wounds, but others were conspicuously unharmed. He grunted in satisfaction – some of them had been wise enough to restrain themselves from joining the battle. Perhaps Tzeentch had whispered in their ears, warning them of the failures to come. The Great Schemer wove plans within plans; every eventuality was prepared for.

Especially defeat.

'Where is the Grand Vizier?' he croaked as he staggered out of the circle, ignoring the flames that licked at his battered form.

He recognised his surroundings. It was another warehouse, somewhere in the River District – one of Tarn's many properties scattered throughout the city. The smell of sawdust and rotten fish was thick on the air. Empty pallets were scattered across the wooden floors. He could hear the slap of water against docking posts somewhere close by. There would be boats, waiting to take the survivors to safety, where they could plot and scheme anew.

'H-here, coven-brother.' The voice slipped out of the darkness. Weak. Full of pain. The acolytes made a path, and Aek stepped through them. Some bowed, murmuring obsequious pleasantries. Others glared at the fatemaster, as if blaming him for the setback.

That was to be expected. Every scheme set its ripples in the ocean of fate. The coven would splinter, and the disaffected would form their own covens and weave their own schemes. Thus was the glory of Tzeentch promulgated. Thus would the infection spread through the cities of men. Even in defeat, there was victory of a sort. For every grand scheme that failed, a hundred smaller ones might succeed, and in each of them was the seed of greater plans yet.

Tarn lay on a pallet, his body a burnt shell of its former strength. His robes had cooked to his flesh, and his mask was now a melted cage for his head. His hands were weeping, blackened claws. Several acolytes sat close to him, tending to him as best they could; some among their ranks were apothecaries and herbalists.

One of them looked up as Aek joined them. 'He doesn't have long. We've done what we can.' He wiped bloody fingers on his robes. 'The wounds are magical, and our art can do nothing to heal him.'

Aek nodded. That was to be expected. Few in the coven had the knowledge to undo what the mystic flames had done, save Tarn himself. And he was in no condition to do so.

'Your diligence is appreciated. Go now.' Aek gestured. 'The servants of the Storm will be combing the city for any sign of us.' He looked around. 'Remove your masks. Slip back into old rhythms until the call to meet comes again.'

'Will it?' someone asked, half in challenge.

'As sure as the sun rises, and fate claims the unwary,' Aek said firmly. He set the Windblade point-first into the floor. 'Go. Now. I would speak with my coven-brother, before the end of his thread.'

He summoned a soft wind to emphasise his point. It moaned through the warehouse, rustling papers and tugging at the acolytes' robes. They left, swiftly, all heading in different directions, careful not to let anyone see where they went.

Aek waited until the last of them was gone. Then, he sank to his haunches beside Tarn. 'You've looked better,' he said.

'So have you,' Tarn croaked. He reached up and caught Aek's wrist. 'Tzanghyr is dead. I can feel his soul rotting in me. It saps what is left of my strength. And when I perish, we will both be truly dead.'

Aek nodded. 'I suspected as much. The Stormcast did something. The crooked path is closed to us, and all those on it, lost.'

Tarn closed his eyes. 'Lost,' he muttered. 'All lost.'

'Regret is the spice of a life well lived,' Aek said gently. Part of him – that part that was still human after all these centuries of service to the Great Schemer – mourned the wreck of a man before him. Tarn had sacrificed much, raising the stakes with every gamble, and now it had come to this. Somewhere, the gods were laughing.

'You've said that before,' Tarn coughed. 'Vetch is dead.'

Aek nodded. 'He came to the end of his thread. As Tzanghyr has. As we all must, in our own time.' The names of those who had slipped from ambition's path were legion. Tzeentch's game was complex and ever-changing, and every gambit had its sacrificial pawns. This scheme had failed, but new ones would be born from the ashes.

'And when will you come to the end of yours, Aek?'

Aek was silent. He had often wondered the same thing. But it was useless to worry: Tzeentch would preserve him until he chose not to, and not a day longer. His grip on the Windblade tightened, and the sword groaned.

Tarn laughed weakly. 'Never mind.' He patted Aek's hand. 'You must walk the path alone, now, as you did before you joined us.'

Aek stood. 'Yes,' he said. 'Goodbye, coven-brother.'

'Goodbye, Aek. And good fortune.' Tarn closed his eyes.

Aek raised the Windblade in both hands. It moaned eagerly as it slipped into Tarn's heart. The magister shuddered and died. The glimmering motes of his bifurcated soul, entwined with that of Tzanghyr's, rose with the Windblade as Aek extricated the sword. He reached out and gathered the motes to him, as he had so many times before.

Nine hundred times or more. He had lost count now. With every setback, his strength grew, just as Tzeentch planned. Wheels within wheels. Every eventuality was planned for. Especially defeat. Soon, his strength would be enough to tip the balance of the board and secure victory when it was most needed.

'You were wrong,' he said to the flickering motes. 'I have not walked alone for many centuries. And I will not, so long as you and all those who came before are with me.' He pressed the motes to his chest, and felt their warmth as they became one with him. 'Together.' A rush of possibilities, of fates unwritten, filled him, and his aches faded. 'We are all but facets of a whole, pieces in a game greater than any of us.'

He lifted the Windblade, and he felt the hands of his coven-brothers on the hilt. It was lighter than ever, and he wondered to what purpose it would next be put. Only Tzeentch could say. For now, Aek would simply go where the winds blew him.

'The greatest game.' He smiled. 'And one we will surely win, in time.'

ABOUT THE AUTHOR

Josh Reynolds is the author of the Horus Heresy
Primarchs novel *Fulgrim: The Palatine Phoenix*,
the audio dramas *Blackshields: The False War* and
Blackshields: Red Fief. His Warhammer 40,000
work includes *Lukas the Trickster*, *Fabius Bile:
Primogenitor*, *Fabius Bile: Clonelord* and *Deathstorm*,
and the novellas *Hunter's Snare* and *Dante's Canyon*,
along with the audio drama *Master of the Hunt*.
He has written many stories set in the Age of
Sigmar, including the novels *Eight Lamentations:
Spear of Shadows*, *Hallowed Knights: Plague Garden*
and *Nagash: The Undying King*. His tales of the
Warhammer old world include *The Return of Nagash*
and *The Lord of the End Times*, and two Gotrek &
Felix novels. He lives and works in Sheffield.